What Gets Into Us

For Jeremy — I hope you — With all my best — Love in New Orleans — We loved having you near —

Moira

March 2007

What Gets Into Us

Stories by Moira Crone

University Press of Mississippi Jackson

www.upress.state.ms.us

The University Press of Mississippi is a member of the Association of American University Presses.

The following works have appeared in journals and anthologies:
"The Ice Garden" in *Triquarterly*, Spring/Summer 2006.
"White Sky in May" in a different form, as "Aunt C's Arm," in *Louisiana Literature*, Winter 1999.
"Mr. Sender" in *Image*, Winter 2003–2004, no. 41, and in *New Stories from the South: The Year's Best, 2005*, Algonquin Books of Chapel Hill.
"Salvage" in *Shenandoah*, Fall 2004, vol. 54, no. 2.
"Where What Gets Into People Comes From" in *Ploughshares*, Fall 2000, nos. 26/2&3, and in *New Stories from the South: The Year's Best, 2001*, Algonquin Books of Chapel Hill.
"It" in *Natural Bridge*, Spring 2006.
"The Ice Garden" was the 2004 winner of the William Faulkner/William Wisdom Creative Writing Prize for Novella, sponsored by the Pirate's Alley Faulkner Society of New Orleans.

First Edition 2006

Library of Congress Cataloging-in-Publication Data
Crone, Moira, 1952–
  What gets into us / Moira Crone.— 1st ed.
    p. cm.
  ISBN 1-57806-772-3 (alk. paper)
  1. North Carolina—Social life and customs—Fiction. 2. City and town life—Fiction. I. Title.
  PS3553.R5393W47 2006
  813'.54—dc22

                                2005025715

British Library Cataloging-in-Publication Data available

For Kezia and Anya, my inspiration and my joy

My thanks to those who have been there, close at hand: Rodger Kamenetz, Marc Bregman. And to Joe DeSalvo and Rosemary James, the royalty of New Orleans readers.

I am also grateful to Jon Gregg, Louise Von Weise, and Gary Clark of the Vermont Studio Center in Vermont, for their generosity in hosting me several summers while I worked on these stories. And to the English Department and Louisiana State University for their support while I completed this book.

I am indebted, as well, to the wonderful editors and writers who have given me support by selecting my work and encouraging this book along the way: Gish Jen, Susan Firestone Hahn, Patty Friedmann, Greg Wolf, R. T. Smith, Kenneth Harrison, Janette Turner Hospital, Kathy Poires, and Shannon Ravenel.

I am also thankful to Seetha Srinivasan, at the University Press of Mississippi, an amazing presence in southern letters and publishing, and to Walter Biggins, who has been my guide.

Contents

The Ice Garden

Claire McKenzie, 1959

I

You could see it in her eyes, he told me—her gaze was more translucent, more liquid. What he wanted me to see was the proof she was better. And I was trying to see it.

She came from the past, from a time when people could be more exaggerated, he said. Yet she would catch up. She could be modern, his Diana, now that she was home from the hospital. She would live with us again, be our mother. It seemed to me to be all he talked about.

In part, she was more willing to please. She did things she'd never done before. First week home, she went to the beauty parlor, let strangers take off half a foot of her hair. They tugged on her head, wrapped her platinum locks around rubber sticks like crayons. When she came home in a taxicab—they weren't letting her drive—I thought she looked pitiful, like a startled poodle. But to my father she was lovelier than ever. And because that was true, things would be all right. He promised me. He believed.

. . .

During the second week she was back, I heard him arguing about the treatment with Dr. Blaine. "They gave her shocks up there. Was that necessary? Was it?"

Shocks were like being struck by lightning on purpose, I knew that.

"You signed the papers, Connor. It had to be," the doctor said. "Look at this straight on, would you?"

"Of course I will," my father said, his chest filling.

• • •

Right before Labor Day, she even tried to make iced tea the way Aunt C had done it. Aunt C, that she'd "sent packing" in the spring—that is how Mother referred to the way Aunt C had to leave. It wasn't quite like that. Someone else had to pack for Aunt C that day she left. She couldn't pack for herself after what happened.

My mother drew me into the kitchen. She smelled wonderful up close, a scent that surrounded me, entranced me. I'd forgotten. "You have to help me, Claire," she said.

I was only ten, but I knew how. I told her to use eight bags in two cups of boiling water. Once you had the concentrate, you put in the sugar. That was the way Aunt C had done it. Then you diluted it with water and ice. She did what I said, as if she were the little girl. But when she actually tasted the tea, she grimaced and stuck out her tongue and bit it. The sweetness hurt her teeth. She said that in Fayton they drank tea sweeter than they did in Charleston where she grew up. But she was going to do things "the Fayton way" from now on. "The way your daddy likes things," she paused, swallowing again, shaking her head. "So, this is how your daddy likes it?" There was a certain face she made, as if the whole world was hard as could be to be in. She made me feel that way too, when she looked like that. After she asked me that question, she began to pour the entire pitcher of bronze liquid into the white sink.

But I said, please, please, let me have some. As if just because my mother made it, I would like it.

It was worse than the pure Coke syrup we had to drink when we had colds. Even so, I took it right down, to please her. Then I gave some to Sweetie, my baby sister, who actually did like it. Our mother said Sweetie didn't have sense. She always said that about Sweetie, or something worse. She never did stop doing that.

. . .

September. Dora Cobb down the street was turning five. Her parents—Tulip, her father, and Isabel, her mother—were having an open house for the grown-ups along with the birthday party. It was a big step, to try out the public. I told Sweetie I had the heebie-jeebies, but she didn't know what I was talking about.

As soon as we walked into the Cobbs' wide bungalow, I couldn't take my eyes off my mother, and neither could anyone else. She was more amplified than other people—rounder, taller, blonder. She had bigger, prettier eyes. She looked slightly like Marilyn Monroe, actually, but her features were finer—none of them were pudgy or girlish or soft. My mother also had talent. She used to play the piano, very well. But my father said it got her riled, all that pounding, so since she'd come back, she'd given it up, too, at his urging. He claimed this was a wonderful sign.

I knew she missed Chopin. The music calmed her down, especially the sonatas that swung from hard to soft, from high notes in cascades down to low ones. When she played the piano she hummed, which made it seem she was content. So I did believe that something beautiful could cure her, if only temporarily. I held out that hope, for the most part. I still believe in the cure of art, in a way. But at that time, when I was a child, I trusted that my father was right: it wasn't going to be Chopin for my mother. It was going to have to be something else.

In Fayton, other grown-up women wore shirtwaists, or flat wraparound skirts, or, if they were daring, capri pants, with oxford shoes or tiny flats. They all dressed more or less alike: Cheryl Sender's mother, Olive, my friend Lily Stark's mother, Eunice, Isabel Cobb, who always took the most care about her appearance, which my mother said was too conventional. Knowing what to wear was very much at the center of things then, in a way I think people can not conceive of exactly anymore. The crucialness, I mean, of looks. I like to think that since those days we've backed away a bit from that, given women something else to do besides "look," which really means "be looked at." But sometimes it feels as if it's only gotten worse.

She wore a party dress to the party, not sportswear. When she sat down and tried to chat with other mothers, she didn't use a couch the way other people did. She had a more interesting way of doing it, of tucking one leg under the other, of spreading out her skirt. As if the couch were all hers, as if no one else in the room even mattered. And I was proud of her for this in a way, this abandon: when I was with my mother, no one else *did* matter, not really.

It was the world to me to sit on her big skirt on the Cobbs' couch, and sink into her side. It would have been fine if we'd been alone. Or perhaps, even better, if we'd been up on a stage on that couch, or in a live tableau in a department store window: Mother and Daughter in party dresses, something to behold.

But at the Cobbs', I knew I had to keep my ears open. I had to be there, I couldn't just be on view. I knew that other people existed, and that the way my mother had of telling the truth upset them. Once in the past, she had told a woman her baby was yellow and asked why. She once told Dora Cobb's father, Tulip, that his brother, Honey, ought to be sent away because his mind was feeble. It probably was true but nobody said it.

During this particular birthday party, she sipped tiny sips from her cup, and nibbled on the small corner of the huge white cake Dora's grandmother made, and hardly said a word.

Isabel Cobb, whose black hair was all curly around her head, so she had "piquant looks," according to my mother, faint praise, said to her at one point, "Diana, I just think that hairdo is perfect, just perfect."

"Oh, is that what you think, Isabel?" she said back.

Like my mother, I didn't agree with Isabel, actually, but at the same time I knew my mother should have acted grateful. That was the thing that you did in public. I didn't correct her, but I knew that was a difference between myself and my mother: I knew it, if I was with people and I said or did something wrong. My mother didn't know, or didn't care. I have never been sure: she's been gone so long now there's no way to find out. Most of the time now, in most of my moods, I assume it was the latter. But I don't always think that.

When we got home from the party that day, she exploded. It was a great effort, controlling herself at the Cobbs', she told me. Other women looked at her funny. They regarded her with awe and worry, at once. But I didn't say that. I didn't want to hurt her.

"Isabel was making fun of my permanent," she said. I said, no, no, no, she wasn't. But then my mother pulled at her hair, and I could see her scalp getting red. I couldn't stop her. This was one of those times when she didn't feel pain at all, when she was so in her own world she couldn't even imagine the idea of pain, anybody's, when she took the side of the demon who hated everybody, her self most of all. I grabbed her hands finally, but not before she pulled patches right out of her scalp. Two clumps of blonde, there on the parlor Persian carpet. I grabbed up the hair and threw it in the trash: it would trouble my father so much to see it. But I couldn't do anything about her head, the horrible little spots of bleeding.

"It isn't working, and I don't see why it should," she went on when I got her in the kitchen. Got her to sit down. "They all dress like miniature, unhealthy men, as if they have something to prove."

She was a little better then. I'd made her some coffee the way she liked it: black as tar, and hot, and she said to me, "Listen, don't you do that, dress like that. You could be pretty. And you should dress to be pretty because what else is there?" She gave me her shallow laugh. "Have you had a single thought about your complexion today?"

I had heard this before, as long as I could remember, how my whole life would be decided by how pretty I turned out to be. And I had to concern myself with my complexion, my skin, my weight, my clothes, my posture, every day even now, in fourth grade. I didn't know then if she meant this was good or bad, that you had to think about these things so much. I suppose you could say she was a person who advocated for a condition she only barely endured: the condition of being obsessed with one's exterior, one's beauty. I almost knew it was not a life she always liked, the one that beautiful got you, the one that staying beautiful created for you. She complained about all the taxing routines: sunbathing, pin-curling her hair, doing her nails, refusing to eat this or that because it made you fat, doing her eyes and her lips over and over and over in a single day. Yet she never wavered in these rituals. She insisted on the sovereignty of good looks in all things. My father insisted upon it too. He was the one who had the absolute faith, the unwavering conviction in her beauty. He was the true devotee.

. . .

I cannot recall her ever saying I was, or would be, "a beauty."
She hinted sometimes to me that this might happen, that I might
wake up and when I looked in the mirror, it would have come to
me, my special beauty, but she wouldn't tell me for sure, if or when
it was coming. So I was always, then, waiting, in anticipation, for
that word, for that power. I would lie down in bed sometimes and
have fantasies about things I knew nothing of—boys, movies,
backseats—and I would always begin them by saying, "On this
night in the future, when I am beautiful . . ." Then I would
describe to myself exactly what I would be wearing—sportswear,
expensive sportswear, usually, but occasionally I would dare to
imagine a real party dress with a wide skirt and a cinched waist,
the kind my mother looked gorgeous in. I'd conjure myself in
such a dress. But I was never sure that it would happen, that the
night when I turned beautiful would ever come. In a way that
whole year I was suspended, in waiting, I think sometimes, and
then I tell myself not to think that.

After I gave her the hot coffee that day, after I listened to her
rant about the Cobbs' party, she invited me into her huge closet to
show me her grand dresses, the formals, the ones for real dances.
Tulle underskirts, no straps. She asked me to stuff the crinolines
into old hose, so they would keep fresh for the next party. She
insisted these dresses had to be preserved, although she hardly
went to those parties anymore, the kind where there was a huge
dance band, white tablecloths, rum and Coke, and dinner.

I was close to her on the closet floor. Her tuberose perfume was
especially strong. The job was like forcing blooms back into buds.
When we were done, the stuffed hose were scattered about like fat,
severed legs. She didn't put them back on the shelves above the
hangers. I wished she would, they bothered me. She started to tell

me stories. What things were like back when she was happy dur-ing the war, when those officers flocked to her. I had heard these before: romantic stories very like the ones I made up when I was going to sleep. Not one suitor, two or three or more. I could listen to her forever, I thought.

But when I went to bed, the tuberose scent surrounded me, and I didn't know if I could breathe. It kept me up for hours, until finally I had to take a shower to get rid of it. I was afraid someone would come find me, shout at me to go to bed. Ask me what I was doing. Find me out.

I still stayed up, after the shower, wrapped in a towel under the blanket after bathing, listening to the night radio. Little radios, transistors, were brand new then, and I could take one with me to bed, let it talk to me on my pillow. I loved that. There was a hurri-cane in the Atlantic, I remember, and I couldn't sleep until I heard it had made a turn, that it had gone out to sea.

• • •

My father didn't ask much of her. Most of the time she could do whatever she pleased. As long as it was nothing much, that is: lounging, getting dressed, doing herself up, talking to the maid, telling her what to do. He was absent a lot—at the office all day, as that was where a white lawyer from a good family, in a small Car-olina town, was supposed to go. But it was also true that he was the only one who watched at all, who kept things, as Aunt C said when she was still around, "afloat." Or that's what I believed then, of course, that he was the source, the steady one, the solid man. There was some sort of family boat that could always sink, but he would save us, wouldn't he? My baby sister and I were the cargo, the ones who could fall out, but he would never let that happen. He was supposed to be the one who kept us in.

• • •

I heard my parents talking on the side porch in early October. My father was asking my mother to pay more attention, take on more responsibility. Since she was well now, he said. She was well, except that she'd pulled out her hair that one time, I thought. But that permanent had fallen, and she had her loose movie star hair again, held back from her wide and impressive brow, with little fancy bobbie pins. And I hadn't ever mentioned her fit after the Cobbs' party. I thought of it as just a lapse, an error, and she had told me not to, to keep her secret. I held all her secrets, then. Every one.

"You are letting things get out of hand," he said to her. He was talking about the household, about what should be bought at the grocer's, what kind of meat loaf should be made, what sort of desserts. "Sidney doesn't know what you want. You have to tell her. Talk to Isabel Cobb, get some ideas."

"I have nothing to say to Isabel Cobb," my mother answered. "I don't have any small talk. I never have. Small talk is as far as she goes."

It was true, I thought, listening. Nothing was small to my mother. Why should anything be? I thought.

"I try, do you have any idea how hard?" she added.

"But you criticize everybody. Never see the good. Look at them as if they should have come from Charleston."

Fayton wasn't like Charleston, where she came from. The thing about Fayton was that everybody knew everybody else. You didn't live only your life, you lived the whole town's life. In cities people didn't do this. In cities—Aunt C had told me, she was from one—people lived by themselves, or families by themselves. She had told me I was lucky because I had the town, my friends, my teachers, the neighbors' mothers, and Sidney, our maid. That all of them would keep me safe, and raise me. She told me that the day she left. She stopped to tell me that even in the midst of all her trouble.

"I don't want you to be anything, or make any small talk," my father pleaded. "I want you to be happy, is that so hard, Diana?"

I could have told him the answer to that. But this was back in the days when I would tell him things, and he wouldn't even know I was speaking, he was so focused on her. I would tell him the same truth right now: for some people being happy is too much to ask.

. . .

Aunt C was the last of his family she turned her back on. She was a widow, with no children of her own, from big Washington, as we called it, because there was also a little Washington, the one up near Elizabeth City, North Carolina, near the Albemarle Sound. She came after Sweetie was born, because Sweetie was just too much trouble, my mother said. The year she spent with us was the best year of my life so far.

Aunt C knew what we needed. She listened to us and played games with us and read to us and made food we liked. We *were* hers, and we wanted to be hers.

I heard Aunt C speak to my father frankly once not long before she had to leave: "I don't want to hear it, Connor. I've heard it. It was a war, and she was beautiful. And you had to have her. Well, now you have her. So what are we going to do? Don't lie to me. Don't lie to yourself. The children deserve more. I don't care what you want to believe. It doesn't matter what you *hope*."

I recall there was a long silence, after that. I don't recall my father having an answer, after that.

. . .

A few days later our mother said Aunt C was stealing our love, which belonged by blood to herself. Only to her. She shouted at all of us, including my father. After some resistance, he must have decided to believe her.

I didn't understand how Aunt C could be a thief.

Two days after that, he came knocking on my bedroom door early in the morning, to tell me that Aunt C was hurt, though she would get better. But she wasn't staying. When I asked what happened, he said she stumbled on the stairs, on one of Sweetie's shoes.

One of her soft little shoes, I thought. Soft as a sock, I thought. How was that, I thought.

Outside in the hall, I heard Aunt C crying behind the closed door of her little room. When I tried to go in, she said, "Go away, go have breakfast. You can't see me like this." She said she'd be fine. She said my father should leave. "Tell him to go on, what is the use of him? Let him go off to the office." He did go a bit later— he seemed ready to do that, eager, in fact. As if things were fine, as if things weren't about to sink.

"How did you fall?" I asked Aunt C when I returned to her room with some bacon, after a breakfast where my mother only stared at me, wouldn't speak.

I thought Aunt C would smell the bacon—she loved it—and open the door, but she still wouldn't let me in. "Is that what they told you downstairs? That I fell?" she asked.

I pushed my way in then. She was still in her old lady nightgown. Swiss made, like mine, with a bib, and sleeveless. She was darkly bruised on the neck and wrist. She was drenched, and weeping. I thought, how much water could be in her? Even her hair was wet, and not from a shower, from sweat. It was terrifying to see a woman that old that you loved, crying like a girl at school. She smelled a fright, like iron mixed in with lavender. Her one arm was covered with a shawl. She wouldn't lift it to let me see the worst places, where her shoulder had been wrenched, where she'd been thrown down, where the arm had nearly been pulled from the socket.

"Will you do something for me?" she said in a tiny voice. "Call Cheryl Ann. Tell her I have a little job for her, will you do that for me?"

I did what she asked, using the upstairs hall phone, and then returned, sat on the edge of the bed watching Aunt C on the vanity bench, and waited for Cheryl Ann Sender, a neighbor girl in junior high school. She lived down at the end of the block.

That's when Aunt C told me how I could trust my place, my town, and the people around me, my father, too, she said, "Although sometimes he's too idealistic, darling." My mother called from the hall outside the room, "Don't help her. Come to me, Claire. Don't you see what she's been doing? What a liar she is?"

Aunt C reached over and put her good arm around me. I didn't pull away even though I knew I should. Finally my mother went downstairs to play music.

Cheryl Ann was the oldest girl on the street. My mother had already designated her a beauty, but I didn't despise Cheryl Ann for that. I worshipped her. After my mother had stopped hanging around in the hall, and started pounding out Chopin, I sneaked down to let Cheryl Ann in. Cheryl and I helped Aunt C go out the back way, on the servant stairs. Sidney saw us, told me my mother said I wasn't to leave the house. All by herself, Cheryl took Aunt C to the hospital where they put the cast on. That's when Dr. Blaine got involved. Later that day, Cheryl Ann came for Aunt C's clothes. She packed them all up in two plaid suitcases.

It was all over by six. Aunt C was gone in a taxicab with Cheryl, straight from the hospital. She left on the night train, so shaken she could hardly walk.

The next day, Dr. Blaine came by the house and spoke to my father in the library, and said it had to be. My mother had to go to the hospital. He didn't say what kind. I heard that later, when Sidney was talking on the phone.

The hospital for people not right in the head.

. . .

There were big state hospitals then, with nice grounds, which were peaceful, some of them—people lived in such places for years, their whole adult lives. Families could take a person there and drop them off. That was, to their minds, the solution, although my father never thought in those terms, I don't think, of a problem and a solution. He had hope. It was always a sweet idiot hope that things would be something else, not what they were. Sort of presto, like that. I tried to correct for it, and also, I half-believed him, but young as I was, I knew he didn't have it quite right. I didn't want to know it, though.

These other families didn't feel terribly guilty about it. They didn't wrack their brains, when they dropped someone off. I've been told stories since, ones that don't end like this one does.

These big asylums were condemned and shut down later, and such people were put out to be with the rest of us, in grim apartments, and so forth. But there was, in the past, another way of doing things, and in a sense, people could go on.

They put my mother in a red brick building up near the state capitol. Her room had barely any furniture. There were tight white sheets and a thin blanket on the bed, which had a hard metal frame—silver, cold. She was there all summer with no air conditioning, just a box fan. My father took me to see her once. He didn't take Sweetie. My mother didn't want to see Sweetie, he said. That didn't seem to bother him.

When we got to the hospital, she cried and asked why we

wouldn't let her come home. And I cried too, a great torrent of tears, for I felt several things. I felt as if I were in some way the cause of her being there. Because her fight with Aunt C, her attack on Aunt C, was what had caused her to come, and Sweetie and I were the issue in that fight. I felt enormous loss with Aunt C gone, as well. I felt terrible loneliness. Nothing was all right that summer. Nothing.

My solution was to insist that I stay, keep my mother company. I could lie down next to her, and she wouldn't have to be by herself. I will cure her, I thought, I can. I liked to think I had powers, somehow, that I could do it, all alone. I needed to think that, I suppose. Somehow at the time it must have been a help.

She said she had no one to talk to. I saw that was true. The people in the lounge on her floor were horrible: they picked their noses and beat on the table with their palms when they laughed at the Red Skelton skits on TV.

My father said I couldn't stay, and then he sent me into the hall with those crazy people. He closed the door, and spoke only to my mother, in low tones. I believed also that, inside there, he was kissing her over and over and I didn't want them kissing in that white blank room with that cold metal bed, I didn't, I wanted them to stop. I wanted to be taken home, if I couldn't spend the summer in that white room with my mother, lying down beside her on taut hospital sheets. I certainly didn't want my father in there. Sweetie, my baby sister, was at home, and nobody watched Red Skelton at home.

When my father came out of the room he rushed quickly past the people by the TV, and the nurses, and he pulled me down the hospital stairs and outside and into the car, but he didn't say what the matter was. He didn't speak to me at all, as a matter of fact, the whole ride, which was not unusual, but on that particular trip I especially wanted to know what he was feeling. By custom, for my mother always rode in the front seat, I rode in the back, so I was behind him, not with him, even though she wasn't there. He changed the stations over and over on the radio, but as soon as he found a game he liked, and he'd heard a few plays, the sound would start to drift, and he'd have to try again, to find another announcer amidst all that static.

That part of the Carolinas was no radio paradise: there were places the stations couldn't reach even at night, when Fort Wayne, Indiana, and KDKA Pittsburgh could get to almost everyone on the planet, it seemed, except to us. He never asked me what I wanted to hear. I was not, it didn't seem, a real person to him then. Later, I was, but not then.

• • •

I don't know what they said to each other that day in the hospital, not really. I believe they were kissing, but they were also talking. Children never know the true nature of the private negotiations between their parents, the intimacies, but it doesn't seem right, in a way, does it? Since the souls of children are the product of those struggles, their lives are the concrete result. Children should have complete access to their parents' intimate lives, you might argue, they should burrow in and watch them, see it all. But then the whole picture tumbles down, doesn't it, then all the scenery and the facades collapse. And then what: probably what we really don't want to know.

• • •

June, July, and August, Sidney had long hours. There was no one else to watch us. I loved her, but she didn't know what we wanted, the way Aunt C knew. Sidney had a life of her own, and moods, and she was distracted by the troubles she had with her man, Raoul, who often got into fights, or other sorts of troublesome business down at a place called the Golden Parrot. I always thought of it as the only nightclub in Fayton, and it seems that they had liquor there, although Fayton was a dry town in a dry county. But somehow everything that happened there happened to people who were drinking.

I do remember that she told me about the blues, that summer, and what to do with them. She must have seen something in me. I was not entirely in a good way that summer, or that fall, for that matter. I was becoming a little odd, a little separate, I could feel it, although I felt no power to stop it. Sometimes when children came up to me and said something about my family, I burst out in a sweat, and I ran to a grown-up. I'd had words with Lily Stark, my neighbor two years younger, whom I had played with the most—I could have no more to do with her. The teachers always took my side, for I was Claire McKenzie and I was somehow already special. That was becoming my defense in life—that I was superior, exceptional, unlike the others, the rabble.

After I came back from seeing my mother, Sidney told me I had the blues, that I'd had them for months, in fact, since the business with Aunt C, since my mother was sent away. Sidney had been shy with me before, but that day she took pity, I suppose.

"When they come, you just shout them down in your mind, taunt them, say, 'Hello, what you got for me today? Think I can't take it?' Like that," she said, "and they scat."

"They do?" I said.

"Well, sometimes they scat," she said, then she kissed me, which was rare. She smelled of baby powder, and bergamot. She was slender, straight, young, and tall. "Maybe not every last little bit," she amended. And I started practicing, shouting down the blues in my mind. I did it all summer. I did it for years. It is effective, up to a point.

And then, late August, when my mother came home, my father said, "Isn't this wonderful? She's cured." When he said this he was looking very handsome. And I couldn't think of anything better than having a beautiful mother in the house. In a part of myself I believed it too, that she was cured. That everything would be fine, fine, now that we had her back. Now that I had a mother.

I wouldn't be eleven for several months. In certain ways, not all, I was still simple.

. . .

The third Monday in October, Sidney left a pot of grits unwashed in the sink when her ride home came to get her, and my mother started screaming. The next day it was chilly, and Sidney wore a sweater to work which was unbuttoned three down from the neck. When I showed her, for I was very conscious at all times of what everyone was wearing, Sidney buttoned herself right back up. She said the sweater must have shrunk in the wash. It was a thick knit, with a wide band at the bottom. Because of her long waist, it didn't go all the way down to her skirt. But she had something underneath that, a cotton shirt. No skin was showing, not a bit.

Later that day after Sidney fixed herself, my mother told me to watch her, because she knew Sidney secretly wanted to go out with my father. "What was she doing all those months when I was gone?" she asked me.

"Nothing," I said. "Cleaning."

"What do you know?" she said. "What are you?"

To me the idea was completely absurd. Sidney was a young colored woman, I thought, that was the awful word we used, always, we said "colored." And where was she going to go with my father if they went out? Nowhere. The Golden Parrot was only for colored people as far as I knew, and maybe the white sheriffs who came to rough the customers up.

Black and white people couldn't do anything together in the world that I knew of, except black people could work for white people and white people could sell black people things on time, or arrest them. For the way we lived, what I had seen, this was the entire truth. It was as if my mother were saying that at night trees get up and walk around, to say my father would take Sidney somewhere on a date, and she would want to go. Yet I had to listen.

My mother could see the doubt in my face, but then she explained, her long lashes lowering, that these things happen in the real world, outside of Fayton, and then she mentioned Charleston.

As soon as she brought that city up, she sounded the way Sidney and her friend Zachary who preached did when they were at the kitchen table discussing Abraham or Moses or Methuselah or King David. My mother seemed to think everyone in the world knew the names of people in Charleston, and, like people in the Bible, all they had done was of great importance. Gilbert Crane, for example, left his wife and children for a high-yellow concubine, she said, and took her to Barbados.

I never found out if Gilbert Crane was my uncle, or my cousin, or my great-grandfather, or no relation at all. I still don't know what century any of this happened in. She'd never taken us to Charleston, so that we could get the history straight.

I changed the subject away from Gilbert Crane and his misdeeds. I asked her if we could go down and show everybody Sweetie. It might be nice to take a trip, I thought. Maybe we could see the beach. Maybe the ocean would calm her, the way Chopin did. And it might make her feel better about Sweetie, to see her people fondling her, saying she was a pretty baby, was what I was really thinking. It wasn't that far to Charleston. The way Mother talked, it was in a foreign country.

"My people would eat you and Sweetie for breakfast," she snapped. "You have no idea." She had a husky voice, for she was smoking a lot those last days: Parliaments, or Bel Airs, and sometimes her voice and smoke were in my mind almost exactly the same sad, low thing. Sometimes when I heard it I cringed. I did just then. I didn't want to be that kind of daughter, the kind who cringes at her mother's voice.

My mother's family were Huguenots, I had been told. Even much later, when I was in my teens, if I heard the word, I thought of big, blonde, southern cannibals. Munching on young girls for breakfast, with muffins. Big teeth sinking into slender ankles, dainty pinkies flying up. "Is it a 'she'?" they'd ask, for I knew that in Charleston they ate "she-crabs," especially. Knowing the sex of something was a prerequisite to the delight of consuming it, apparently, in Charleston. He-crabs weren't as tasty, somehow.

In truth my mother's kin were dark trollish people with bug eyes, whom I never felt comfortable around, not for a second. I met them at her funeral, later that year, right before Christmas.

They seemed to have almost nothing in common with her, and they saw her as a stranger among them, a platinum swan among crows, an inexplicable anomaly. As far as I could tell, from an early age she had been sacrificed for her gifts, despised for them, as well as paraded around, pampered, forced into a kind of false perfection, exploited. They all "adored" her, they told me. She was their precious, their gorgeous one. "And spoiled," they said. "You ever seen spoiled?" As if that were the delight of her, and why she was a menace, both. They had once had money and they had come down out of it, they hinted. But this was all very vague in 1959. People had erased their old lives by buying ranch houses, by having many cars, and doing a lot of moving around, but there were references to mansions, to streets in Charleston, to rot and beetles and high water that had come for these assets over the years, and left them in ruins—left them, in their hearts, utterly desperate people. Or perhaps they had always been desperate. It seemed as if they were all standing in front of a vast gulf in the earth, something gaping open. They were terrified I would see it. When they spoke to me one shoved himself in front of another, so I wouldn't see the chasm behind them, and they marched toward me, one trying to out-explain the other, concealing the awful truth that would not leave them, that they were terrified I would see. One did not have to see it. It was enough to see how they felt about it.

. . .

My mother wanted to fire Sidney. Through the late fall, night after night, they fought about it. My father insisted Sidney had no designs. He wanted her to stay on. I felt the same way but no one asked me. There was too much to do without her. My mother wasn't good at certain things. I had seen her try, but she couldn't do them, nobody had ever shown her. She was used to the world doing for her. She couldn't sort Sweetie's tiny clothes, for example. Or clean up the nursery. She was no good at cooking—she knew absolutely nothing about it. Even iced tea was a struggle, that was proven. I wanted to weigh in, but of course I couldn't. Even if I had spoken, they would not have been able to hear me.

They settled it that Sidney could only be there when he was out of the house. My father said that was how my mother wanted it. And that was how it would be. This seemed reasonable to him, something we could do, put up with.

They took up this plan right after Halloween. I still wasn't sleeping well. It wasn't the perfume anymore. It was noise, my parents arguing. I stayed up late, listening to Ft. Wayne, Pittsburgh, Havana on stormy nights, WABC in New York City. A fall chill came on suddenly that week. Arctic air, swooping down into the

Carolinas, the weathermen said. There was no in-between, just Indian summer heat, then a hard frost. The trees hardly had time to change. In a few days, some were blaring color, and, as quickly, bare. This will be the pattern this year, they said. Hot, then freezing cold, they said.

In the end, the winter took us by complete surprise, which was why the wood was so brittle in the storm, in December, people said, why the damage was so severe.

. . .

I woke the Saturday before Thanksgiving to the sound of Sweetie crying. It seemed far away, almost in another world, but that could happen in that house. There were seven bedrooms, two parlors, a library, a butler's pantry, two staircases, a sleeping porch, and a room just for the piano, which was locked.

I went to the nursery, but Sweetie wasn't in her crib. The bathroom next to it was empty. As I got closer to my parents' bedroom, way down on the other end of the hall, I heard water running, but no Sweetie. Mother must be taking a bath, I thought. So Sweetie got into something, I thought. But where did she get to?

My parents' room had a big sky-blue chenille bedspread and heavy curtains. There was a chaise lounge, peacock satin, with little fleur-de-lis in the pattern, where my mother spent much of her life with her cigarettes. The bed was unmade, but no one was in it. She usually slept late: for her to be up on a Saturday before nine was a surprise. Then, it was silent. I even thought I had dreamed Sweetie's crying for a moment.

But I heard her again. A different sound, like a goose. Honking. I wondered was she in the hall, caught on something. I was afraid of the bath because my mother would shout at me for sneaking up on her in there. And she must have been in there, for the water was pounding away.

Sweetie screamed again, and so I had to venture in. First there was the vanity room, with two sinks, and a wide mirror. The tub was in a room beyond that. I turned toward it, sure I would see my mother's naked body, which was smooth and wonderful, under bubbles. I had seen it before, how perfectly white she was. I had seen her high breasts through the steam.

But I found Sweetie in the bath, by herself, on her back, naked, and red as a kidney bean. She was flapping her arms, and her little mouth was opening and closing. The water was up to her ears, and rising. I lifted her by the arms, and then I almost dropped her on the tile floor. She was so heavy, and slippery. But I got her head over my shoulder, which changed the distribution of the weight. She stayed put for a while and I managed to get a towel around her. Sweetie was a thick, heavy baby I loved to be close to. Even when she was squirming across my body like that, her lungs wide open screaming, there was something wonderful about holding her. Everybody was supposed to want a lusty baby like Sweetie.

Struggling down the hall with her, I saw my mother below, standing on the first landing looking out the stained glass window. She was wearing a satin quilted robe, and had a cup of coffee in her hand. I knew that this act, the one she had just committed, of leaving an eighteen-month-old alone in a high tub with the water running, was terribly wrong, and was no accident. But how could that be, I corrected myself. How could she leave Sweetie in the bath? Sweetie must have got in there some other way. Although I knew no other way. It was a big, deep tub with feet, and walls too high for her to climb in or out.

My mother must have heard us coming, Sweetie honking in my arms, but she did not turn around to see us. When I got down to the landing, I saw her eyes were veiled even though they were open. She finally said, as if surprised, "What? Oh, you have that thing. She never stops complaining." Then she paused, and I thought I saw a flash of something that frightened me: a glance like frost. She said, "Good of you. So good of you."

Then she looked out the window again. She said in a moment, recovering herself, "Come see, honey, the trees, through the stained glass, come."

I went. I gave Sweetie my thumb so she would stop screaming, but she didn't. My mother acted as if I weren't holding anything in my arms.

At the window, nevertheless, I fell into mother's world, immediately, willingly. How could I believe my mother capable of such things and still live, still go on? I just looked out the window and tried very hard to forget, to reimagine what I'd just seen, to focus on the lovely leaves drifting down, visible through the old, wavy glass. Burgundy red maple leaves, drifting down, ever so slowly.

I was doing very well. And my mother was, perhaps, training me, showing me something, about how she dealt, really, with the world, something she wanted me to know, and I was ready to receive it, to believe in it, I must have been. She was my mother, and this was something she wanted me to have, a gift from her. The gift of reverie. And then she said, "What did you say?"

"I didn't say anything," I said. I hadn't.

"I heard you, what did you say?" she asked again. She was loud, she had to be, over Sweetie, who was still wailing from fright, although my mother completely ignored that.

"I didn't say a word," I said. "I promise."

"I better not hear you," she said. "I better not in this life—you know what's good for you?"

I said, "No ma'am. No ma'am." There was nothing else I could say. I had very few choices with her, and besides, I had to take Sweetie somewhere, get her dry and dressed.

• • •

That night, I started a new routine: I pretended to go to sleep at eight, but then, when everything was quiet, I got up. I pushed my bed against the wall—this was hard to do without scraping the floor, but I did it slowly, gliding it with towels under the feet. Then I went in the nursery. I took Sweetie up out of her crib, and put her between myself and the wall so she wouldn't roll out. I slept like that until first light. Then I got up and put her back, and moved my bed to the center of the room. By then I was usually too awake to go back to sleep. I sat by the window, and waited, with a certain dread, for the house to come alive again, for my mother and father to wake up, for us to get on, as the phrase goes, with our lives.

II

It started coming down one morning in December about six. I noticed it after I put Sweetie back, and then later, when I was watching Sidney out the window. She was waiting for my father to pull out of the drive so she could come in and fix everybody else breakfast. The trees were leafless by then so a person could have a view of the sidewalk from across the street. I was looking at all the houses, trying to gauge if our neighbors knew what my family was doing to Sidney. The ice was transparent. You had to sort of believe in it to see it.

On the way to school, I felt the coldest, windy air, air that made you swallow first and close your eyes, because it didn't seem true. I liked a misty, secret cold. It seemed a great chance, to have a real winter, like the children in the readers had. It felt as if something we'd always been promised was finally being delivered.

I loved school. I loved the cloakroom, the construction paper, the poles you had to use on the windows to open them because they were so high, the stout widows who were our teachers, Mrs. Horn, Mrs. Bailey. I loved it more lately than ever. Once we took off our scarves and caps and mittens and thick coats, it was just a December morning. I didn't worry about Sweetie even.

Soon as class started, I was let out to paint a mural on paper on the bulletin board in the cafeteria. I was known for my paintings, already. Since first grade I'd been doing them in tempera. Whatever the season asked for: witches, cats, hearts, cherry trees, wise men, bunnies. Around holidays I hardly spent any time in class. The teachers all thought I was too smart to need lessons anyway. Nobody had noticed I'd been falling behind since Aunt C left in May. I didn't have my times tables past six. I couldn't study, especially for the last few weeks. I'd been worrying about Sweetie, and doing things Sidney didn't have time for now under the new rules.

I was working on a scene of children sitting on the floor by a tree, a mother above them with a real smile on her face, and a big open book in her lap. The father was looking on with great interest. Behind them was the Christmas tree. These were smooth pink people like the characters in the Dick and Jane books, or in the family TV shows. The mother looked a lot like my mother—her hair, her big eyes. But I remember thinking I couldn't draw someone as pretty as my real mother. Her beauty was too mysterious to capture, to even try. There was no point—she was so far past me.

After a while the first graders came in for lunch. They were all talking about the "stuff outside"—discussing whether it was snow or ice or sleet. I prayed for snow because I'd never really seen a good layer of it. And I thought how I might take Sweetie out and pull her on a garbage can lid with a rope tied to it. She'd go far, she'd slide down hills, we'd sled pure across town.

Around one-thirty the principal, Mrs. Taylor, announced school was let out. The highway department said the roads were freezing up. The cafeteria ladies let me phone home. Asking what the problem was, my mother said Isabel Cobb had called, and offered to fetch me along with the other children. My mother still wasn't driving—Dr. Blaine was against it. So I waited out on the sidewalk next to Bit Cobb, a wild boy, who was throwing wet iceballs, wanting to put them down our shirts, and his sister, Dora, who was in kindergarten, who wouldn't let go of my leg. She was afraid of ice. Lily Stark was there too, smiling at me. Mrs. Cobb came in her big old Cadillac and stuffed us all in the backseat. Even though she went fifteen miles an hour, the car skidded twice, and we all slid in the back from side to side. There were no seatbelts then. Lily squealed and giggled. I couldn't help it, so did I. When she got to Winter Street, Mrs. Cobb said she was glad we were all alive, but we were still laughing.

• • •

At home I found my mother in the living room with the drapes drawn. The heat was on high, and she was wearing a shirtwaist with no sweater. She looked lovely, flushed, and pink. I wanted to hug her, but first I searched around for Sweetie and found her in the playpen.

My mother said, "Is it that bad? I let that bitch Sidney go home. She begged. I told her not to come back. Ever."

"You fired her?" I asked. I couldn't bear it.

"What good was that hussy?" she asked.

I wasn't supposed to answer.

I knew this voice, this old, nothing-is-good-today voice. Hearing it this time, my shoulders rose up, I breathed more shallowly. To myself, I said, "What do you have for me today?" As Sidney had taught me. But my mother looked at me as if she could hear what went on underneath my breath. In a way I wanted her to know. I knew she ought to know my life, she ought to be inside it. But I was afraid she'd hear what I said, how I yelled at my blues the Sidney way, how I worried about Sweetie now, how I sneaked her into my bed at night.

In some way there is no escaping a mother, even when she is gone.

Sweetie charmed me that day, I remember. Sidney had dressed her up really pretty before she left. She had on her scuffed white shoes and her corduroy smock, the yellow of the inside of a pound cake. Fat cheeks.

My mother said, "Look at those bug eyes, she's so plain."

To my mother, love that didn't follow from beauty was somehow flawed, awry. If she saw a couple on the street and the woman wasn't beautiful, she asked my father what was the man doing with her? Did the woman have money?

I confess I felt it a flaw in my own makeup sometimes, how I didn't make a judgment about Sweetie's looks before I fell in love with her. But I had no choice, I didn't care. Besides, she had that tiny little mouth.

My mother said this storm better turn to snow, which was bad enough, but it would be worse if it stayed ice. The trees, she said, the ice takes the trees.

I had no idea what she meant.

She said it happened in Charleston in the thirties, and she went on, telling me how bad things could get. After a while I had the thought my mother was very brave, compared to other people. Because it was so hard for her to live, knowing all she knew, feeling all she felt, as disappointed as she was, as confused and jealous. My mother needed beauty to keep her going. There was just no other way for her. She could never get enough. I must be just like her, I thought, then I thought, no.

· · ·

Drafts were seeping into the rooms, I started to notice. And after a while her words were drowned out by a certain tick-tick-ticking, loud as an orchestra of clocks. "Where is he?" she asked about my father. "Why doesn't he care?"

I knew that he cared.

"I know he can't drive, he doesn't have his chains on," she said.

Chains, I thought. Like the ones on the ghost in *A Christmas Carol*, which Mrs. Horn just read to us. That my father might own chains like those seemed completely true to me, in some way. But I didn't know why my mother would mention it now.

It was five o'clock, and I wanted with all my heart to take Sweetie with me and watch *Sky King*. It was about Penny, who had no mother, whose father saved somebody every week in his airplane. My mother had things to ask me, though. I tried, but I didn't know many answers. Finally she let me go, said I should "go see what that Sidney creature left in the oven."

I walked to the back den where we kept the TV in a cabinet. I could hear the dizzy ticking outside as I went—it was stimulating, interesting, after the heaviness in the living room. I told myself I was happy. Very very happy, in fact. School had let out early. There would be none tomorrow, everybody said.

I could see out those diamond-paned windows that the twilight was coming soon, and it was greenish. The twigs and buds on the nearest trees were gleaming. Icicles were forming on the eaves of the house. Everything seemed dipped in glass. Like varnishes and glazes do to paintings and china, the ice brought all the beauty out, made things more precious somehow. As if everything in the world were getting polished. So it would be prettier. I wanted to show my mother. But she'd asked me to look in the oven.

· · ·

It sounded like a huge giant cracking his knuckles just beyond the back steps. The whole kitchen shook. A great thud, then.

The overhead light died. Out the window I saw our one apple tree, a pockmarked favorite of woodpeckers, had fallen. Aunt C had told me once it was half-dead. I thought of an old soldier keeling over in battle. Then I heard my father's voice, and ran to it.

He was standing in the first parlor, in front of my mother. His cloth coat had white flecks on it, and he had taken off his felt hat. He was medium tall, with a round head, his hair thin. He had been very good looking ten years before, but his features were pliant and small, and the thickness of his face was taking over, his nose and eyes sinking in. Yet I still thought him the handsomest man on earth.

He was talking to my mother about the country house, where my grandmother lived until she died. It was on a small farm that bordered Sweet Creek. We still owned it. We rented it out furnished when we could find a tenant. It was empty that fall, and next door to the county power station. The house was on the trunk line, he said. There was just one empty field standing between the power station and our house.

I didn't know what that was, the "trunk line." Ice and trunks made me think of Hannibal with his elephants, that Mrs. Horn had told us about.

The stove was gas there. There were fireplaces, he said. Our house in town had been modernized, and we had electric heat, so we had no hope here. We could cook there, he said. It is an idea, he said, but he wasn't sure it was a good one because of the roads. The farm was two miles outside of the city limits. He said we could be stranded out there, so, on balance, he wasn't sure.

"Let's go," my mother said. "Let's get out of here," in a tone that meant there was no way around it. And he didn't hesitate. He solemnly nodded. I saw that it seemed to fulfill a great wish that he had, that she would make a decision. That she would be the one whose wants were there for him to answer.

. . .

After stuffing the trunk of the old round blue Ford with blankets and towels and cans and baby clothes, we pulled out of the drive, and edged toward the darkening street. The wheels, which were where the chains were, it turned out, were chiming. I was in the back seat, looking at my mother's pale profile, her high, extraordinary brow.

The town was very dark, but not blue, instead, green—what is called pthalo green in a paint box. I felt a glory in it that night, an attraction—something close to excitement, but higher pitched, more rarefied.

There were no streetlights, and the only houses with any lights at all were those of poorer people on the outskirts of town, on the other side of Sycamore Street, the ones that still used kerosene. The streets were lovely, so dark, the only lights the ones glowing in the windows. They were old fashioned, not rich and modern like us, and used propane in a tank to cook with, and coal, or heating oil, and they were all doing fine, my father pointed out as we drove by. "Mother, the irony of it," he said.

. . .

I was in the back, staring at the two of them: my father with his fading handsome face, my mother in her soft curls, and a beret—the only hat she had for the cold—set on her head at an angle, just so. I knew my mother could walk into a room and people would say in their hearts: somewhere there must be perfection in this world, this crumbling world, if creatures like her can still be produced. I knew they thought that, looking at her. I still thought it sometimes, too.

I wondered that night as we drove out there, how long I would have to wait on my beauty, my real beauty. How long I would have to wait to know my fate. But at the same time I could also wait forever, staring at my mother. I still found her irresistible, the way people who didn't know her found her. I fell in, under her spell. In one part of my heart, all I wanted in this life was to look at her and look at her and look at her. My own mother. I wouldn't want her to do anything, or say anything. Just to be there on view, the way she was in the front seat of the car, the ice-filtered glow from the last street lamps illuminating her wide and open and porcelain face.

My father was also wearing his hat, so his eyes were obscured, but he turned once. It interested me how boyish he looked. He was addressing my mother as "Mother." Later, I would remember this ride out, and how it was the last ride like that anywhere, and I would recall the hope I still had, especially when my father called her "Mother." A boundless, whirling feeling, without end, without even the knowledge of an end. That is what I was feeling that night. That was the kind of thing I could still feel, directly.

• • •

When we got to the old house, my father unlocked the door and showed us into the foyer, and reached for the light. It came on, pinkish yellow, incandescent—this seemed so miraculous. My mother shouted out with actual, rare joy, "At last." Her mood heightened everything, the way a mother's mood was supposed to do.

Heaven, I believe I thought. This will be heaven. We can start over, fresh.

The old TV came on, I was delighted to see. A Zenith, a tiny screen, set up in a box with a phonograph on top, fabric across the speakers on the front.

My father went to the stove in the kitchen at the rear, turned the knob, tried to light the pilot. He sniffed. No gas. He went outside then, through the side door that led to a brick-paved mudroom. Coming back, he said the line into the house was still there. The gas must have been turned off. The last tenant hadn't been gone that long, so he was surprised.

"It's a valve, go turn it on—worry about the company later," my mother said. "It might freeze over by morning."

"Well, where is it?" he asked her.

He must have known, somewhere, that she wouldn't know the answer to a question like that. But he listened to her. He needed to, he couldn't help himself.

"Somewhere in the ground by the road," she said. "It must be." It was a country place, set in at least a quarter if not half a mile from the highway. The property was ten acres across the front. The valve could be anywhere, but she was right, it was near the road, so the workmen could adjust it without driving up to the house.

By then my father was setting up an old hot plate beside the useless stove. It was starting to heat, turn orange. He spread his palm above it. "Yes'm, right away, right this minute." But I knew he wasn't going out into the freezing dark. He was rebelling against her, finding his little outlet, I could see that.

My mother looked at me as if to say, "What's that about?" She seemed like anybody's mother, irritated by her husband's obstinacy, wanting allies. I thought her wonderful, at this moment. The way he did, I suppose.

We ate the roast we'd brought, what Sidney had cooked. This was fun, we were camping out. But we weren't going to start any fires in the fireplaces. There was no wood. My father said that was a job for the morning: flues to open, chimneys to look at, broken branches outside to chop. He seemed to be looking forward to these jobs. It was already eight-thirty. We'd go to bed. The house was cold and not that many rooms had lamps. We put what supplies we had in the refrigerator and my father set Sweetie and me up in the back room, by the TV.

He seemed happy that night. He seemed so certain of us all that night. I was certain too, that we were fine, afloat. Or almost certain.

Then they went upstairs to the main bedroom.

I lay under a quilt for close to an hour. Sweetie beside me on the wide old couch, something from the nineteen forties. I was listening to the noise outside. We couldn't get any TV stations by then, just static. The show was outside. Branches breaking, shattering ice exactly like shattering glass, loud as a war in a movie. The noise was amazing, catastrophic. I was so tired I was dreaming awake, watching marching giants falling in the forest, one, then another, then another.

Later, in the patches of silence between the sounds of crashing trees, I heard them talking through the grates in the ceiling. I felt invaded. I didn't want to know those tones anymore. I could feel them like little claws in my chest. I shouldn't have been so happy, I chided myself. Then these things wouldn't hurt so much.

"You can just try, you can. You have tried. But I can see now," he said.

My mother said, "What do you think you can see?"

My father said, "That you are giving up. That you are going down. That you don't care."

"God, what else do I do but care?"

She did care, I thought. It wasn't easy for her, I thought.

"You are giving up," he told her again. "Why? Why?" Pliant, begging. There was something in his tone I hadn't heard before. A sinking in, a sense that they were nearing the bottom, the falling-off point.

I told myself the things I was always telling myself: that she was trying. She just wasn't that good at life. She had to learn. We were all going to show her. I tried to resurrect my optimism from a few hours before: perhaps not this fall, but tonight, surely tonight, we would start over, and she would learn. But then there was more crashing outside, more giants tumbling in the forest. They wouldn't stop. I couldn't stop them.

. . .

When I woke, sometime later, I didn't know how much later, the room had a strange glow to it. It had gotten very cold, and the sconce in the hall was off—it had been on when we went to bed. So the power was gone here, too. The night now was just the night. Our plan, her plan, was wrong, had failed.

Yet I couldn't help a certain, secret thrill in me. A curious thrill that didn't have anything to do with anybody else. The crashing had ceased. My parents weren't talking. Nobody was talking. The night was able to shut down one time, not bothered by all that buzzing, buzzing around. Talking, worrying, making plans, fixing what was wrong. Listening to see was someone crying or hurt, where Sidney was, where Sweetie was, who was angry, who was calm, was my father home yet. The empty quiet was precious to me. I couldn't hear anything but Sweetie's baby breathing. Which was all I wanted to hear, which was the best sound in the world.

I remembered years before, the first time I'd felt the same, or something like it. The calm, I mean. I must have been about six. This was before Aunt C. My mother had gone for a walk, but she hadn't come back. Not for hours. All afternoon, she was gone, and it was just Sidney and I in the house, and an everything-is-all-right kind of silence. I remember I sat in the parlor and looked at the clouds, how they passed over the sun, and every time one came, and the parlor darkened, I told myself the clouds were hours, visible, and gentle, and lumbering. We wondered where she was, Sidney and I did, but we were just wondering, in an idle, lilting way. At other times we'd called my father, and let him know, and he'd gone out looking, but this time we didn't tell.

A deputy sheriff found her, brought her back like a stray. She had gone out of town past the tobacco fields south of Fayton, past the wooden homes with the pinwheels in the yards and the tar-paper-covered barns and shacks, the poor people's farms. He'd found her on a red clay bank beside a single-lane road, he said.

Lying there in the emerald dark, I remembered how she looked when she was returned to us. Captured like a wild thing, coming in and stomping on the pleasure of the afternoon, destroying it. She didn't want to be with us, I knew it, even then.

I knew that living lacked mostly all savor for her, except when she was in one of her rages, or humming to Chopin, or when she first saw something beautiful. She especially liked things so extreme in their beauty you might call them spectacular or ugly. Beauty like that. Nothing else. Nothing in between. And nothing sentimental. Beauty did hold her. She was desolate without it. But mostly she did not find it. The kind she needed was very, very rare. Practically, you would think, impossible. Sometimes I think I have spent my whole life since trying to find that rare beauty for her, the kind she needed. She left me with her craving for it.

• • •

From above, I heard her say, "I will not. I won't." It seemed especially final to me.

And my father said, "Well, then, that does it."

And my heart sank. Heaven had been so close that night.

"Now, in the middle of the night?" she asked.

My father saying, "Yes, yes." He wanted to go back. He felt we'd be too isolated. Back to the house in town.

"I'd rather die," she said. "I would. I would rather die. Do you hear me?"

That is what she said. He heard her. So did I.

"I would rather die than go back to that house."

She said it three times.

. . .

When I got up about five, I could see my breath. Sweetie was still sleeping, making tiny baby snores. I went into the bathroom to try to flush, but it didn't work. Pipes frozen. So things were worse. I wrapped her in a blanket and found the room behind the kitchen, the one with the brick floor. From there, I looked out upon my grandmother's old formal garden, in that first light.

The sides of the garden were still defined by boxwoods not trimmed in years, but they grew very slowly, so they still held their shape. In the center was an oval bed of tall, hard-leafed camellias, pinker than any roses. Each was coated in ice, hard as china flowers. At the back there were two beds for bulbs with brick boundary walls two feet high, and beyond that, a stand of dwarf pines, weighed down by ice: green princes bowing for me, I thought.

Past all that, something spectacular. I could only catch a glimpse. Open land, which was the clearest blue-white, a dazzling splendor of ice. It was the brightest world I had ever seen. It was almost too bright to see. I felt pierced by the part of it that was visible, and I longed to go into it, to see it all.

I heard my mother then, coming up behind me. She said, "This place is lost. All the trees will have to come down. Come over here, look." She pointed out the grove of pecans at the back of the house, the ones with the sweetest meats. There used to be a whole line of them. A seventy-five-year-old grove, good bearers, now desperate amputees. She showed me the ugly mess, the destruction the storm had brought. I almost said to her, *but look at that field to the east, that pure field of ice. If you want to see something beautiful, you'll come see that, with me.*

I was going to say it. In fact, I think everything would have been different, this would be a very different story if I had said it, if she and I had taken a walk through it, but when she touched my shoulder, came near me with her tuberose scent, I pulled away. I cringed. I went looking for my father.

In the shallow fireplace in the downstairs parlor, using wood from freshly fallen trees, that was too wet, that bled reddish sticky sap, he was trying to start a fire, and getting nowhere. Sweetie was on the rag rug in front of the thing, having the last of the milk. "Well, this is it," my mother said. "There is no way out."

She seemed to enjoy saying that, taunting him.

On the transistor radio I heard there was no school from way up in the mountains all the way to Myrtle. In the piedmont of the state, in the stately part of the state—those dignified places as I thought of them then, with winding roads and slight hills—they had snow. Fayton didn't rate that. Fayton was just a federal disaster area.

Later on, my father found two men from a mile up the road to help him move the car, which had frozen where he'd parked it. They gave him some sand in bags, a great treasure, and they pried his Ford from the ice. He came in after, around ten, red in the face from his exertions, his long walk, to announce that he'd heard there was coal to be had, and that the main highway was passable.

He said he was taking me.

He never took me, before, like that.

It occurred to me that if I went somewhere with him, if I was alone with him, I might do the right thing for once and he would see me.

But also, I couldn't be gone so long without Sweetie.

"I might need some hands," he said to my mother, justifying himself. He had his sand, he said, and flattened cardboard boxes. He might need help putting these under the tires if we got stuck. For traction, he said, looking at me.

"You will not take Claire, are you mad?" my mother said. "All kinds of dangers are out there—power lines, treacherous streets, thieves."

"It's Fayton," he said. "What are you talking about? Let her come. Christ." The same rebellion from the night before.

"No, I won't let you take her," she said.

"I am," he said, in the way that meant he was. He hardly ever used that tone with her, but there he used it. She shut up. I noticed that, and it satisfied something in me.

"Make her sit in the backseat," my mother said.

"Why?" he asked.

"It's safer when you have a wreck," she said.

He said fine, I would be in the backseat.

"It's okay. I'll stay," I said. "I'll stay." I didn't want to go without Sweetie.

"Listen, you come, Claire," he said. "Go get your car coat and some gloves, you have gloves?"

When I was in the back room, bundling up, my mother came to me and said, "Tell me what he does. Tell me where he goes. Who he talks to. He doesn't tell me. He lies. He always lies."

"Of course," I lied.

I checked on Sweetie before I left the house. She was sleeping under a thick quilt, on the floor in the parlor between pillows. I told myself she'd make it.

"If you are late, I'm calling the highway patrol," my mother proclaimed as we walked out the door. "Do you hear me?"

I heard her, but I didn't answer her. Neither did my father, which thrilled me.

. . .

When I got outside to trek toward the car, the frigid air bristled in my nostrils. There was an alarming, emergency scent in the air. Like a constant panic. I knew it was the sap of all the broken trees, especially the evergreens. The pine pitch, the smell of green. It was inescapable, it pounded in my head. It was a scent that said something, like that iron with lavender in Aunt C's room said something. *Pay attention. Don't drop your guard.*

As soon as he closed the door on my side, I wanted to climb out of the car, and go back to the house, because of Sweetie, but I wanted to be with him, too.

My father inspected the chains, which were still attached to the tires. And then he got in, and we started to roll, clanking along like escaped prisoners, slowly, noisily, around five miles an hour. In spite of all, I couldn't contain the joy of this ride, the thrill of taking off like that with him. The danger of it, too.

On the other side of the cinder-block Pentecostal church, about a mile down the road, was a grocery. This was a country store beside a slaughterhouse I heard my mother once tell Sidney not to buy at. She said it wasn't clean like the IGA, but my father stopped there because, he said, "It's open. We can't be choosy." It was the first thing he'd said since we'd left the house.

I had never seen him grocery shop. I wished Sidney were with me. I thought she would laugh.

First he got cereal and paper towels and paper plates and a huge bag of boiled peanuts. I followed behind him and grabbed candy. This didn't bother him at all—he didn't seem to know that candy was different from food.

Then he thought of Sweetie, and he turned into the aisle with the little jars. Anything with a Gerber face on it, that goofy baby, he put it in the basket. She could eat food from the table now—this had been true for months, but I didn't say anything. It was amazing to watch what he did, how he thought. I was hardly ever alone with him, except at church, and there he never said anything but the prayers.

We swung by the meat, and he took a look: a butcher appeared and waved his hands back and forth. He meant to say, the cooler is out, forget about meat. I bent down toward it, and I knew at one whiff the contents were rotting.

My father went to the left, and grabbed some bags of dried beans. I wondered if he even knew what to do with poor people's food.

Someone said, "Well, Connor, remind you of the Depression?"

"Just the same," he said and a smile crossed his lips. "Except I can buy the butter beans."

His accent was thicker than normal, I noticed. He sounded like one of the boys at school who wore blue jeans, which were country. The boys I thought about.

We neared the back of the store. There must have been six or seven men sitting around smoking, by a stove that squatted in the middle of the floor, a stamped metal plate below it and another up at the ceiling where the pipe went through the roof. When I had been in this place once with Lily Stark and her family's maid, Pauline, the stove had been half-hidden by bread displays and potato chip racks, and covered with dust. But today it was resurrected, wiped down, and stoked with wood. The people around it were so hot they were sweaty.

I took a Baby Ruth and just started eating it. I prayed he

wouldn't see. But then he did see, and it didn't matter to him. Not one bit. He was too distracted by the business around the stove. He knew everyone's name. He shook a few hands. They started in on practical matters: the coal, if there was enough on hand for all who needed it, and wood, who still sold wood in half cords, and could you get to the people with firewood in an old Chevrolet with chains.

I marveled at the sound of his voice, the way it moved around words when he talked to people, as if there was pleasure in them by nature alone. And at the way he cleared his throat to change the subject, the way he whispered something to an old man and made him grin. It occurred to me that if I hadn't been there with him, reminding him of his errand, he would have stayed until nightfall.

Someone with an apron told me I could wash down the candy I stole with milk. It was bound to spoil soon—I could have as much as I wanted, free. While I was getting a carton, I heard my father make a noise I'd never heard. I wasn't sure what was wrong with him. When I ran back—drinking from the spout like a common person, but I didn't care—I saw he was sitting beside an old man in overalls and rubber boots and he was laughing. It wasn't his high light laugh he did around Mother, the one he used for Jack Benny on TV. It was very deep. It was the warmest thing he had ever done in my presence. I sat on the floor and watched him listen to the old men who had storm stories and Depression stories and kept telling, over and over, versions of the same ones—how one froze, how one starved, how one thawed, how some, not all, came out alive.

Finally, after I'd had a quart of milk and two Baby Ruths, and taken a few for the ride—and he'd filled up on peanuts he hadn't paid for yet, and wouldn't—he looked away, said we had to go. It was maybe three-thirty. The cold was coming back to stay the night, we both could tell it. The sky was getting almost pink. Above that, a layer of green, hovering, as if in wait.

This time I got in the front seat. He forgot to tell me not to. I felt so special sitting there, next to him. I would feel that way with him many more times, all the rest of my girlhood. When I grew up, I held onto this specialness. It is very hard to let go of.

We drove slowly through the ways of the town. These were fresh, blue-green frozen paths, carved out of downed trees, draped power lines, between the old shoulders of ice-covered Fords and Dodges and Chryslers, parked or abandoned cars that hadn't been moved, and now couldn't be. It was strange to be rolling along when everything else was so still. To me the whole world had stopped so we could get a perfect view.

We came to a place I knew of but had never been to. Bryer's coal yard. He worked here once, as a boy, loading coal onto wagons, he said. He'd never told me about his boyhood before, I knew very little. Filthy work, he said, smiling.

There was a huge bonfire in the yard, and thirty or forty people were standing in a sort of line, on the white-blue ice. There was the slightest dusting of snow underfoot, under the ice layer. I had never seen much real snow, so this was a thrill, another miracle. We were on the north side of town, the neighborhood between downtown and the old rail station that hardly saw a train anymore. But the train to Washington, D.C., still came through, the train Aunt C took.

I looked at the station, as we turned in and parked a good distance from the fire.

. . .

Nobody would let me go to see Aunt C off. Sidney held me back, told me my mother said Aunt C was a bad woman. Cheryl Ann went in a cab with her to the station, and then followed her right into the train car, sat her down, got her bags stored away. Aunt C was in so much pain, she screamed anytime anything touched her elbow, the one in the cast, Cheryl Ann told me later. Even if it were the softest thing that touched it—the headrest of the train seat, the conductor's sleeve, she winced.

My mother had broken Aunt C's arm in two places. She had torn the top of it almost out of the joint at the shoulder. Cheryl had told me. I knew that, but I didn't like to stay with it. But I did know it. I knew what she'd done to Sweetie, too, or tried to do. I was still the only person on earth who knew that.

. . .

It was easy to spot Sidney among the milling crowd, tall and elegant in her plaid coat with huge silver-colored buttons. I walked right over to her; I couldn't bear the thought she wasn't coming back. But then, when I was close to her—she looked so pretty, energized by the cold—I remembered what my mother told me, and I ordered myself to be vigilant.

"We will talk about yesterday," my father said. "When we come back. We aren't home. We're out at my mother's old place." It was then I realized it had been just yesterday that the storm came. It seemed forever ago. We had left one house, and settled into another, and I had so much hope, but then they had started in at it again, and my mother had said she would rather die. And now we were stranded, although for a few hours my father and I had escaped. So many things to have happened. This had only been twenty-four hours, but it felt like a concentrate of my whole life, with a slightly happier ending than the one I used to foresee, the one right now, where I was in that coal yard with my father, him holding my hand, which was bare. For I had left my gloves in the car.

I felt very old looking back like this, grown up, seeing things in some kind of perspective—and for a moment I believed I was going to have a new life, that must be the reason I saw everything as containing the signs of coming toward a conclusion. It is a habit I still have—finding meanings in things that may not have them. I know it is dangerous to bury motives in every chance event, set them around in a story, waiting to explode. When in the first place, things happened, just happened. To come up with reasons for everything gives a single person too much power. And I have been trying to stop doing that.

The truth is, that afternoon, I also thought of my mother, and my mission. I know I looked at Sidney's face to see if she was in love with my father.

"You all gonna freeze out there?" Sidney said.

"Four fireplaces, coal, I don't think so," he said.

"Sweetie okay?" She asked me this. For, of course, Sweetie.

"She's with her mother, she's fine," he said, clearing his voice. And in a certain way that was new I could feel the lie of it he had to always tell, could see how it lowered his eyes, turned them darker, not so light gray. I felt horrible for him. I wanted to leave. We had to leave. I did realize that. Of course. This might be heaven, but we didn't live here. We were stranded out at that house. We were gathering coal to bring out to that house.

All through the frozen streets on the way home, I stared out at the stalled cars, like statues, under collapsed branches, covered in treacherous ice. I thought of what I wanted, which was to get home, but also to never go home, to stay with my father forever in town, and to get back and give Sweetie some of the milk I'd stolen, maybe a piece of a candy bar. I wanted so many different things, I wanted nothing. I didn't want to be anywhere. I wondered where I could go, wanting that. I opened the last Baby Ruth I had and started pulling the peanuts out of it, so Sweetie could eat it without choking. But in the cold of the car, my gloveless fingers were too stiff and the candy was too hard, and then it dropped on the floor by the front seat, and that seemed the most terrible thing I'd ever done, dropping that candy, taking this ride with my father. I never should have come. I was sure something had happened to Sweetie.

In the hall when we got there, my mother held a match up to his face, and then to mine, and said nothing. She was a wreck: her blonde hair matted, no lipstick, no eyebrow pencil. She frightened me. She was so mad she could spit.

It was bitter cold in the house by then. I could not believe we were inside. I looked around, immediately, for Sweetie. My father put the coal in the grate, in the shallow fireplace in the front parlor. He wadded up the grocery bags, and lit them.

Eventually, there were a few hot places in the room. I thought my mother's fury was over, she'd been silent so long. My father went upstairs to try another fireplace. My mother had forgotten about dinner, or had never had a thought of it. I got up to fetch the milk for Sweetie.

My mother followed me out into the hall and grabbed me by the arm. It wasn't gently. I felt my heart tighten, like a fist in a box.

"Tell me something," she said.

I tried to pull away.

"What did you and he talk about?" She was hard on me. She talked to me the way she talked to Sidney. She hadn't done that before.

"He used to work in the coal yard," I said. "He told me that. When he was a boy."

"What did he say about me?" she asked.

"Nothing." Knowing exactly how that would anger her. "Did he ever tell you that?"

"Say nothing, ma'am, who do you think you are talking to?" and for a moment her lips turned in, became very small. It was almost like a trick, how she made herself so ugly that night. "Why did you keep him so long? What did you tell him?"

"I didn't tell him anything. Ma'am," I said.

"I saw you riding in the front seat," she said.

"I wanted to see things," I said. I waited a very long time. Then I said what she wanted, "I'm sorry."

"You aren't sorry," she said. "You say ma'am, you hear me? You have that right? Even when you are lying like a little bitch you say ma'am."

I waited again. Now my heart was moving around in my chest. It had come out of the box. I didn't say ma'am. I didn't say anything. I was against a wall, so she couldn't push me down. I thought of that.

"Well, little girl?" she said, mocking.

"Yes ma'am," I said finally.

"You know what's good for you?" She raised her hand.

Something just as hard as her words was about to force itself out of my mouth. I didn't even know what it would be, only that it would be terrible, but my mother turned and stomped up the stairs, calling to my father, saying, "What you gonna do about that child, how she talks back, Connor? Why in hell don't you do something ever? Do you have any idea what I have to live with? How spoiled she is?"

"What, Diana?" he said, in his coaxing way, in his way when he wanted to calm her. In his pliant, yearning way. He didn't say I was okay, or Sweetie. He didn't say he loved us. I thought he should have said so.

When she was gone, I was shaking.

• • •

I got the baby milk, and crawled under the thick afghan in the parlor, one my grandmother had made, and I pulled Sweetie in with me.

For a long time we lay on the settee, staring at the fire. Praying they would go to bed. I must have slept some. When I woke again the fire my father had made was only embers, and the parlor was getting too cold. I could hear car tires spinning on the ice. Out the parlor window, I saw my mother lit by the car's headlights. She was standing in transparent booties that covered her high-heeled shoes—the only boots she had—she had no practical clothes. She was in two coats—a fancy mohair, and over it, one of my father's for the rain. She was yelling at him, "What are you going to do then? What? You are leaving? You are going where?"

My father: "Don't you trust anybody?"

"Why don't you do something useful like turn on the gas? Find the valve, it's under a cover in the damn ground."

"I'm trying to get this thing parked. So I can get it out in the morning if it thaws. If we need something." The car wasn't moving. He was digging deep ice grooves under the tires. The grinding made a great noise, the engine revving up again and again, not getting anywhere. It was as if it were winding over and over and over again in my own body. I could not ignore it, or them.

That is why I decided to walk with Sweetie to the small mud room on the other side of the kitchen. It was at the back of the chimney, not up on pillars like the rest of the house. There were two doors, opposite each other, the one to the outside and the one that led to the kitchen. Both doors had glass lights. The screen doors were in a corner: they'd been taken down. Earlier that day, I had discovered it was warmer—the sun had come in, and heated the bricks on the floor. In the morning there would be the beautiful view, the garden, first, and beyond it, the bright, brilliant field.

But I could still hear my parents outside. My father: "When

have I ever not tried? When? To do the best by you? When? How?"
My mother: "Turn it on, that's all I ask. You just want to get away.
Take them, I don't care. GO."

· · ·

There was that word in my consciousness. Gas. My mother had
been yelling about gas, in the frozen yard with my father. "All
right, all right, for Christ's sake," he shouted back. The car door
slammed. She was silent. His steps, marching away in the noisy
ice.

· · ·

When I woke up the second time, I smelled fierce smoke. Then
I saw it coming for us. I don't know why, but the feeling I had was
not surprise. It was a kind of recognition, that was all: here it is, it
has come, something like that.

Out of instinct, I covered Sweetie's nose. Then I crawled on the
floor toward the doorway that went into the house. I could look
through the kitchen down the corridor to the parlor. Smoke was
creeping through the hallway toward us, flowing like a flood into
the kitchen, and rising. I could see this because of the light of the
fire, beyond, in the parlor. I didn't think to close the door to the
smoke, to the kitchen. I left it standing open.

I stood to look out the glass lights of the door to the outside.
There I could see the garden. I tried to open it, but it was as if
some pressure from beyond it held that door closed, some pressure ten times as strong as my body. I threw myself against it, over
and over. Sweetie was on the floor by my feet, the smoke moving
at us, rolling in from the kitchen.

· · ·

I know I looked back and saw my mother's figure walking, not
running, not crawling, in the hall beyond the kitchen. I heard her
for the first time: "Sweetie? Claire? Where are you? Where did you
go?"

Just as I was going to answer, a sweeping-in draft closed the door that led to her. And the outside door swung in and the glass panes in it crashed. The force that closed one door opened the other. The fire, pulling in air. Our way out was clear. I tumbled with Sweetie over the sill, a few steps into the garden. Then I paused, and stood holding her. She was limp and dear as a doll, and not on fire. And I was not on fire. We both could breathe.

I ran with her to the far end of the garden and put her down in one of the old flowerbeds with a brick border that would fence her in. Then I looked back and faced the house. All the downstairs rooms were involved; the parlor was burning. The kitchen was still all right, but darkening. The smoke cleared for a moment when the flames pulled up with the new air.

That's when I saw my mother a second time within. She was a shadow, stumbling. It was clear she didn't know the way out, or couldn't see her way to it. If she'd just get down on her knees, I remember thinking, she might have a chance. She is so proud, I remember thinking. I did think all those things, those normal things. *She won't crawl, and she should.*

Later they told me that happens in fires, people lose their minds in smoke, can't make a simple decision. That this can't be helped. No matter what they know. No matter who calls to them, tells them what to do.

But the fact which is mine, and always will be mine is this: she called me.

"Claire? I can't see. Connor? Claire!"

I felt something hitting my head and face just then: icicles melting off the trees above me in the fire's heat, crashing down on the frozen camellias, the coated boxwoods. Solid shards catching light, dazzling—crimson, cadmium, oranges, even flame-blues. Reflecting the fire, and cold, gloriously cold.

I didn't answer her.

Turning, ducking my head, I glimpsed the open field past the garden. The one that had been too bright to see in the morning. The moon was shining on it, and above I saw the clearest, most extraordinary sky. All was luminous and purple-blue. An entire field of ice, under a river of stars, and beyond it all, at the horizon, broken trees like brushstrokes, the slightest, whispered difference between sky and earth. I bent down under the dwarf pines, took a few steps into that field, for it was beautiful. My mother would love to see this, I know I thought that. But then I thought something else: it belongs to me, just that gesture, that self-encompassing gesture, and is that evil or is it natural. I still don't know.

It felt as if the ice came up to me. It crept from the ground to my slippers, then to my calves in my leggings, then my nightdress and my car coat, and my grandmother's afghan that I was still gripping around my shoulders. It covered me, a transparent gleaming. And for a few moments, moments that mattered, of course, I could only stare out of the ice all round me, at the ice around me. I couldn't move, or save my mother, even call to her. I was just part of that cold place. And in some way, as just myself, I didn't actually exist. I had existed to save Sweetie, but Sweetie was saved, and now I was that pure beauty. As I remember it, I was filled with a mysterious calm, full of charm, of distance.

There was a kind of inevitability to things after: how my father came up to me later, wretched with all his sorrow, and fell on his knees, declared me for all intents and purposes his new queen. How I saw he had to have one, and even pitied him. How we were in some ways happier, after, in our grief, than we had ever been with her. How that became our terrible secret.

I usually tell all this with an eye to its music, its hard, just chords, its Chopin—I am still in that ice garden. It is once I turn, for I am still trying to, trying to have feeling in life the way other people do, that I lose that eye.

When I come back to myself and take a look, the house has no doors, no windows. It is only burning light, against the sky. A thing that can take a body whole, for fuel. A thing that could melt the trees, the ground, the sky, the stars, but it doesn't. I would rather die than resist, but I stay apart. At the same time I don't know what kind of girl I am saving. I believe my mother knows, she must know. I am part of her, and I want her to tell me.

But she is always out of reach. She is always in there, burning.

White Sky in May

Lily Stark, 1959

One time before, we saw heaven. I'm not telling a story.

Then, this May on a Saturday, I took my red bike to Claire's. We stood outside. High as a tower, their fir. Me and, beside me, Cookie. We leaned my bike on the trunk. The earth below, smooth, burgundy brown, smelled like Christmas. All the girls on the block had married Cookie for pretend one time or another. But he kept with me the best. He knew to look out, to not wag his tail, even. We came down to see why Aunt C was keeping Cheryl Ann Sender there all morning. At Claire's and Sweetie's.

Back end of second grade Aunt C came all the way from Big Washington to look after Claire and Sweetie. When she brought Dahlia, a girl boxer, with her then I thought that meant Aunt C would stay and Cookie would find true love. Dahlia was a pretty dog with a square nose. And with Dahlia, Claire and Sweetie would be all right. But Cookie didn't love Dahlia. Dahlia chased cars and barked at too many people. He still roamed. She didn't know a good grown-up from the other kind. So Aunt C kept her behind the fence.

Claire was my best friend once. All that people had to say about her mother, we didn't get around to it. If we were walking to school or even in my daddy's drugstore and there were some words, I took her hand and we just went on or went outdoors. I was younger than Claire, two years, but I acted right so she liked me.

Cheryl came out on the McKenzie porch after a while, said, "I have to stay with her." Aunt C. "She needs somebody to get her to the hospital."

I loved Cheryl Ann Sender. She was fourteen and three-quarters, and lived next door to me. She spoke Latin if she had to, sometimes to us. She was perfect at everything she did. She taught Claire and me and Cookie the North Carolina state motto, even made Sweetie listen: *Esse quam videri*. To be rather than to seem. Not to lie about what you are or what you love. And the one for the Marines, *Semper fidelis*. Stand by no matter what, be faithful.

Aunt C showed up at the screen door, her eyes peeping out from under bridges. The next thing you know she was there by the tree herself. Close up she was saggy and damp, like somebody ought to dry her off. Then she rolled up her sleeve. So we could see it: her wide shocking arm. Cookie seemed he was trying to say something. I couldn't. It was too horrible. Claire and Sweetie were on the porch, then. They stared same as I did. Looking at the two of them, I saw eyes flat as lakes, then Sweetie crying, as if she'd spilled.

Claire wouldn't cry.

Cheryl came down to lead Aunt C back to the door, but Aunt C said, "Let the children see what that woman did in the daylight."

By that woman I knew who she meant.

It was as if Aunt C's whole shoulder was painted with gentian violet. Round and raw, swollen. "Tore it right out of the socket," Aunt C said, and Cheryl said to Aunt C, "Come on now we have to get down there, Dr. Blaine said he was about ready."

Dr. Blaine was going to set Aunt C's shoulder, Cheryl said, down at the hospital. He'd been by the house a couple hours before. I thought maybe Cheryl had spoken to Dr. Blaine in Latin. She could do anything. She was teaching herself French. She had on an azalea pink blouse, with her skinny arms poking out. She had shaved under them one time that I knew of. That took care of it. But her boobs were getting huge. I felt sorry for her over that. I could see her vaccination. She came up with Aunt C's big purse and she started to lead Aunt C down the sidewalk for the hospital. It was five blocks. Mrs. McKenzie's car was there, but I knew she wasn't taking Aunt C, since she's the one who sent her.

Aunt C's eyeglasses hung down over her bosom on a lanyard and she always wore the same dress or one just like it. She never did anything mean to anybody. Cheryl was gentle with her, but they had to move on. She was hardly across the driveway with her, when I realized Claire's mamma was just inside the house. She stood behind the screen door, and you could see her blonde hair and all her makeup for the daytime. Red lips.

"Claire, you bring Sweetie inside now, you hear what I say?—"

I had never heard her call them from the yard before in the daytime. She used to always be sleeping. They had a maid who did the calling, Sidney. She was a friend of Pauline, who took care of me. Before she had Sidney, she had Alberta, that Claire's mother said stole.

Sweetie's face was dirty. Nobody had tied her shoes. Sometimes she was scared of eating, but we would find her something, sugar cereal. Claire was like me, I said, except two years older: flat bangs, ready on her bike, a wondrous speller, missing her dog teeth. On top of how she was just like me, she could draw. I mean really draw, I told her. We didn't talk about her mother, ever.

"Come to lunch, you and Sweetie," her mother said, like nothing was going on in the drive, like no old woman was wailing in her housedress, being led away. Mrs. McKenzie had never made lunch before that I knew of. I would have liked to see it.

Claire looked right at me. I knew her. I knew when she was going to say something, even sometimes what it was. I thought she was inviting me to lunch, and I was wondering what her mother would make, and if it was a good idea to eat it. Cheryl had got to the sidewalk. They had to walk. Like they were poor people. Aunt C was carrying on, and leaning on Cheryl so Cheryl'd like to fall down. I could have gone to help them.

But I was waiting on Claire, under the fir. My hands were hanging on the handlebars. I was not sitting on the seat. I was standing. Dahlia was inside the fence barking. Dahlia was always inside the fence barking.

Claire and Sweetie's mother was beautiful. She hated things when she was up and around. She told everybody about it. You didn't get in her way. She played nocturnes on records or the real piano in the day and the night. She loved Chopin and she might do anything. She was not the only grown-up like that, they were all over, but she was the worst that I knew of.

I had seen what I came to see. Where Cheryl was, what she was doing. What the commotion was with Aunt C. I thought I'd better tell Cheryl's mother about the hospital, that that's where Cheryl was.

When they got to end of the block, I could still hear Aunt C. I mean yelling and she never yelled. I couldn't hear her words but I figured what she was saying: she wanted the whole neighborhood to know.

I could have told Aunt C nothing ever changed once you were a grown-up. No point telling the world what they do. I could have said that back end of first grade when she showed up to help out while they waited for Mrs. McKenzie to change. There is no changing grown-ups. All you can do is grow up and then you get to be one. There is no better about it. I could have saved everybody a lot of trouble, this trouble, but I am too young and people say I tell stories, and get in the way.

Dahlia was still barking. Maybe we could teach her to scare off Claire's mamma if she came after anybody else, I thought. Dahlia was a stupid dog from the city but maybe I could get Cookie to teach her if I put him up to it.

"Claire and Sweetie," I said, "why don't we go down?" I meant come with me.

I didn't know what Claire would say. I usually could tell but not this time.

"Watch how they put on the cast," I said.

Claire got bug-eyed. She said, "Mamma said Aunt C better go back to Big Washington."

Plenty of times Claire and I had gone down on our bikes to the hospital, gone in the back door where Cheryl and Aunt C were headed, and bought fireballs at the candy stripers' shop, three for a penny. The hospital was the end of the places we could go without asking. It was against the rules to go in, but we did it.

"Aunt C was stealing us from Mamma," Claire said. We didn't talk about her mamma, I told you that.

After we got down there, we could stay gone. Live in the back-yard under the arbor, at my house, or in the shed at the back of the Cobbs' house where Cookie slept. Under the house, maybe, except there were snakes under the house. We could live in the park, in the gazebo, or go to Washington to live with Aunt C, in a little house stuck next to another one the way Aunt C's house was. She'd showed us pictures. That's what I was thinking I'd say next.

I said to Claire one more time, "Come on, bring Sweetie."

Claire and I are so alike people think we are the same person if they don't look close, but Claire said, "My mamma loves me and she loves Sweetie too. Mamma loves us the hardest way there is. Do you know what that even means?"

She looked nothing like me right then. And like she didn't know me.

Cheryl and Aunt C were in the second block now, their voices far away like moans, in the light past the heavy trees, growing tiny as they moved. I said, "You remember that man on the table?"

We saw him in the hospital where we weren't supposed to go.

"Mamma wants you to go on," Claire said, saying *you*, like it was something I'd done, being Lily Stark. Like it was something I ought to get out of having to be, and how was I gonna do that even if it was a good idea. "Now go on," she said, and Sweetie was tugging at her the whole time, crying, not making any noise, though. "Mamma hates that mangy dog and so do I. That dog is always hanging around thinking something is wrong when nothing is. Go on."

It was Dahlia who was barking.

One time we went down there to the hospital late in the day, me and Claire. School was about to let out. When we opened the door we saw a table with wheels on it coming down the hall, and two people pushing it. On the table underneath a sheet there was a long thing like a log. Claire said, "It's a body." When the men pushing the table were right up next to us, we held the door wide for them. What else could we do? We couldn't get away. Something snagged—we talked about later what it could be—the belt buckle of one of the men pushing, or part of the hinge of the door—and the sheet came off. We saw the face. Somebody gasped. It was yellow and it was dead. There was a white hearse, from Robson Brothers, the motor running, the back wide open, just outside the door.

I had no other friend like Claire. She didn't like it when you talked about her mother, so we had that rule.

"Look," she whispered to me, back then. "The face, see it?"

The dead person was smiling. You could half-see the teeth. It was probably a grandma, but it might have been a man. It was so old you couldn't tell. Its eyes were not all the way closed. It was like it saw something, up in the sky.

The sky was white with violet veins, like some pansies. And I saw, not exactly in the sky, but in my heart, what this person saw there. Some things are sharper when you see them that way. This is how it was that day because I know it: there is no time in heaven, no days, no months, no years. Nothing happens next. You stay the way you are when you first get there. You don't grow up, or ever turn.

"Go on," Claire said it to me again. "Go on, Lily Stark." Like a scratched record. "Get out of here. Scat."

Claire saw the exact same thing I saw that day in that late sky, she said so. We talked about it. The dead person saw heaven at the hospital door and for a minute we saw it too. It's mostly light purple but there is a golden color that pushes right up to the sides of everything, nearly hidden mostly, but you know it is there. You know it all the time. We talked about it when she spent the night at my house.

"You can't stay at home," I said. "You can't. We have to go. Your mamma—" I couldn't take it back.

"What? My mamma what?"

"Maybe we can see heaven again," I said, thinking how we might get in this time, climb right in from the back door of the hospital, bring Sweetie too, Cookie come up from behind, make sure nobody followed us. That seemed the best plan, the way out. I said, "Remember, let's go."

"You are crazy, Lily Stark," she said. "I don't know a thing about heaven. You are crazy."

Her mamma yelling behind her, her going in to her mamma.

I took off on my bike, to the back door of the hospital. I was going to find Cheryl and Aunt C inside. I had to tie Cookie up by the door, and when I did, I looked at the sky, which was blank, and white. Blank, I already said that. I imagine that this will never change, but I can't do anything about it. It comes to me that my whole life I might think I should go back there and get Claire, and make her come along. It could be something I forgot to do, that never leaves, for everything you missed doing might be hanging around outside this time, asking for you to finish. It could be that way. I am afraid it is.

But I do know there is nothing worse than a white sky in late spring right before summer comes, and everything fills in, so there is no going back to like it was.

Nothing is worse than that.

Mr. Sender

Obituaries, Fayton
June 1, 1963

HAMILTON SENDER, PROMINENT INSURANCE BROKER

Mr. Hamilton Sender, founder and owner of Sender Insurance of Fayton, died Saturday of a gun accident at his home. He was forty-two. Mr. Sender was born in Fayton, and was a lifelong resident of this city. He attended East Atlantic College in Keaneville, and served for four years in the Navy in the Pacific Theater, reaching the rank of second lieutenant . . . Survivors include his wife, Mrs. Olive May Sender, nee Olive Carter, a daughter, Cheryl Ann . . . .

Lily

If you wear a mohair sweater with just about nothing underneath, your daddy will come out on the porch cocking a shotgun. This proves he cares about you. I am eleven years old and I know this for a fact.

Mr. Sender is out there, next door. But Cheryl Ann keeps walking, no matter. It's her reputation that concerns him, I am sure. She goes to her fellow, who is leaning on an Impala at the curb, his arms folded. It is December. Mr. Sender says, "Come back here." I hear him from my bedroom. The fellow holds out a cigarette he's already half-smoked. When Cheryl Ann gets to him, she takes it between two fingers, and pulls on it hard, like it will take her to heaven. I wonder will it.

They drive away. I feel sorry for Mr. Sender, how Cheryl Ann defied him when he was right.

I tell Pauline about this, and her friend Sidney who works for the Senders now. Long time ago she worked for the McKenzies down the street, Claire who lost her mother four years ago. It's when they come back to work after the holidays. Cheryl could have worn a blouse, I say. People can see through the holes in mohair sweaters, I say.

"Men, you mean," Sidney says. "Not *people*. Well, what was she wearing under?"

"A slip," I say. Saw it in the porch light through that loose knit. The color was nude. I know a good girl would never do that. Cheryl Ann used to be good. I don't know what got into her.

Pauline who has raised me says I shouldn't say that word nude. Even worse than naked.

"Maybe she should have worn a blouse," Sidney says. "Washed all her white ones when she came home for winter vacation. Then we wouldn't have had this trouble."

"You probably got that right," Pauline says, but Pauline sounds to me like she doubts it.

. . .

Mr. Sender is spending all his time in his tiny den, Sidney tells Pauline. Sidney's not that used to him. She's only been working over there ten months. She says she told him that Cheryl's off at the college, that she's grown. She says he walked right out not touching his eggs in a fury over that.

"I thought you didn't care about them," Pauline says to Sidney.

"I'm just saying," Sidney says. "What's he doing all day in that den? He writes insurance, his secretary covers the work. But he got to go in once in a while. It don't look right." Sidney has been in the homes of doctors, school principals, bankers. She knows their hours, what little they can get away with. She's always talking about what goes on in white people's houses. She likes to say, *I mean I could tell you a few things, uh huh.*

I can hardly imagine a white man who stays at home. My daddy owns a drugstore and my mamma keeps the books. I am mostly with Pauline. My daddy doesn't see me even if I am standing right in front of him in the middle of the room. Or if he does see me sometimes when he's riled, I wish he hadn't. Mamma thinks I get away with too much. She is certain I am fat. I am ashamed of weighing ninety-seven. Pauline says it's okay if I eat something she makes, her collards with ham hocks, her shelled peas stuck up inside the refrigerator in jars only we know about. Her late lunch, what she shares with Sidney and with me. I know I shouldn't eat the food, but I can't help it. We all sit around and talk while they are waiting for their ride home. I am big for my age, thick on my thighs, and I am starting to need a training bra. But my mamma won't get it. She says I need to live on hard eggs and boiled chicken. I try, but Pauline tells me the opposite, that men love big thighs and I'm going to have me some hams. She pinches me and tells Sidney don't I have a pretty leg, won't I be something. When she says it I smile and think maybe one day I will go somewhere this is true, that men like big legs. Surely they don't in Fayton, I know this for a fact. Here white men like tiny feet and tiny hands, the limbs to go with them. The only thing that can be big is bosoms and girls have to look like Cheryl Ann but not dress like a you know what. She used to dress nice, Cheryl Ann. I used to think she was the finest girl there was. I have watched the junior high girls and the high school girls and Cheryl Ann herself grow up. She was so beautiful in high school she wouldn't have anybody. The man she found in college who came in December in the Impala is the first date she's ever had. He is handsome as all get out, and old, I think, not a boy.

"Thighs are the whole story, you get right down to it," Sidney says, and I say story of what. Sidney tells Pauline to tell me, but Pauline says she can't.

. . .

All this time, this spring, Mr. Sender is inside his den with his rifles for hunting and his pipes and his duck decoys. He never goes out, doesn't shave for a week at a time. Sidney has kept saying, "It's Cheryl, he's pining. He writes out long letters to her he doesn't send."

"He have to let her go," Pauline says.

I have trouble imagining it. A man who loves his daughter, and misses her when she is gone.

. . .

So Palm Sunday is coming on. Everything is early this year. I am standing in the doorway at the Senders' house with a tray of leftover cupcakes from the sixth grade Easter party. On top of each one is a marshmallow chickadee. I might have eaten them all in a single afternoon in front of the TV. But instead I bring them to Mr. Sender, for he needs some cheering up. I know this is Christian of me.

Sidney stands in the Senders' back hall and tells me I am sweet, but she is under instructions from Mrs. Olive not to let people bother Mr. Sender. But then he comes out of his den. He is smiling a little, and wearing a robe and pants, and he says, "What is it, Sidney?" And he grabs a cake off the tray.

"Delicious, devil's food," he says with his mouth full. It is a big mouth, I notice. So is his Adam's apple, and his neck is long. "You the little Stark girl?"

I think of course he must know about me, since I know so much about him. I live right next door. But I say yes sir, because you never tell a man what you think. I know this the same way I know about mohair sweaters and reputations, and the shame of showing slips and wearing dark hose before high school. You tell men what they want to hear. You need to learn that if you are going to get one. I know I have to practice.

The next week Sidney comes over to my house with a present. A stuffed animal for me—it says my name, Lily Stark, on the card. It's from Mr. Sender. It's a green duck with small black eyes.

"Looks to me like a duck he might hunt," Pauline says.

I know why Pauline would say that: she doesn't like Mr. Sender. I am thrilled, no matter. I go upstairs and put a big lilac bow around its neck. One of my own, for my ponytail. Next day I go over there to thank him. This time Mrs. Sender asks me what I want. When I say, she says, "My husband is indisposed. You know what that is?"

Of course I know what indisposed is. I have a good vocabulary.

Mr. Sender comes out then and tells his wife to shut her mouth, and he brings me back into his den. Then he shows me a thing I don't know: what pipe cleaners are for. For going down inside the shaft of a pipe, not just for crafts at school. He shows me about packing the bowl, and puffing on the pipe to get it going.

When I tell Pauline about this time I spent with Mr. Sender, she doesn't see what a nice man he is. She says, "He got guns in there, don't he?"

"He's so lonely," I say. "He misses Cheryl Ann. It is going to be Easter. He gave me a present for Easter. Easter is about loving people and rising from the dead."

"Well, why don't you stay over here in the afternoons for now?" Pauline says. "You do that for me?"

I know this isn't Pauline's business. I say to her, "I don't have to listen to you." When I see what comes over Pauline, how her eyes float and fill, I cry. I won't say I'm sorry. I know I don't have to. I am growing up, and I don't have to. I don't even have to mind her. She works for us.

When I run upstairs I hear Sidney going at Pauline for being partial to me. Sidney doesn't believe in taking up for white people, or spoiling their children, at least to hear her talk. Sidney says I am spoiled and I hear her. Spoiled sounds to me like something that's turned, like milk, then you throw it out. I hate that word. There is no coming back from spoiled.

This is the routine on Saturdays since I turned eleven: my parents go to the store at seven-thirty to open up, while I am still in bed. Pauline goes shopping, and then comes home in a cab with the groceries. She gets to the house about the time I wake up to watch cartoons, sometimes an hour later. She makes me breakfast.

This Saturday the phone rings before Pauline gets there. It wakes me up, and Mr. Sender says on the phone, "So, do I have the little Stark?"

I have dreamed of this call. I have hoped all along he was going to ask for me.

"You want me to show you a trick?" he says.

I get up and put on my shorts and a sleeveless top—a pretty set, with ruffles—and I run over there in my flip-flops.

The Sender house is all open doors. I find him in his den. He's unshaven. His shirt is old and worn, and his head looks too long and seems too pale, but I know I must overlook all that. He looks right at me like he can see all of me. He says, "Did you ever get that duck?"

I think it's odd he's forgotten I thanked him, but of course I lie. He is a man. "Oh yes," I say. "I never told you. I am so sorry. I gave him a bow."

The door to his den swings closed. I see he has one of his shotguns on the leather-top desk. It's not too long. Its handle is wooden. Same one he took out on the porch that night.

He says, "Come here."

And I go.

And then he says, "Watch me," and he takes up his pipe. He draws in a mound of smoke into his pipe with that mouth of his, and then he blows out a ring after a minute. Then he blows out another ring, inside of the first. The two rings float there as if they are doing a dance. This is magic to me. He hands me the pipe. A pipe and I have never smoked. Cheryl Ann took her fellow's cigarette, I know. So I take it.

He says I should take my tongue, and put it at the top of my mouth. Then when the time comes, I do it, with the smoke hovering there, near my palate. Just when he says to, I let it go out from the perfect circle I have made with my lips like he told me. First try, there it is.

"Beginner's luck," he says.

He has seen how I can be wonderful and no one else except Pauline has ever seen that. But I am mad at Pauline. Then he touches my cheek, and he says, "Come here," while I watch the ring, I come there, to him. I see how the smoke is floating in the air, catching light like dust, for it is dust, dirt, and it makes me cough, but I tell myself it is nothing, and I tell myself to look at it. In this light it is beautiful and bluish. I know sometimes you have to ignore things, just look at the bright side. Ladies do that all the time, I know this. Being a lady is all about ignoring things.

And then when I am in his lap, he puts his hand on my waist, and then he puts his hand down under the elastic, and down, way down there. I know he has made a mistake, his hand has gone down inside my shorts, not outside. So I buck my hips up, because this will make his hand slide out without embarrassing him. I know that's the right thing to do, not embarrass him for his mistake. I think I hear someone outside, someone calling me. I buck up my hips, but when I do this, he puts his hand right back. I squirm over a little, and then I look into his face, because I will have to explain to him. I will have to say it sweetly, use a whisper, I know this, that his hand is in the wrong place. I shouldn't seem mad. And when I am about to look in his face, I think, maybe he will say my name and give me a kiss, when he takes his hand out. But when I look up he hasn't got a kiss, just licking. He should know my name. He calls me the wrong name. He calls me Cheryl Ann. Cheryl Ann.

"Be still," he says. "Don't you know what you came for? What is the matter with you? Don't you know? Don't you know? Don't you know?"

Pauline

Everything happens at once, but you have to look at it one thing at a time. That is being alive and it is a shame sometimes. There are several mysteries in this story, if you go through it from one end to the other, event by event. But there is a place you can reach where the mysteries disappear.

After Christmas that year, it bothers me Lily has gossip. She says Mr. Sender next door was chasing after his daughter, Cheryl. Cheryl's eighteen, in college. She can date but her daddy has never liked it. The child says it was how Cheryl was dressed that he didn't like, and I say, "Uh huh, I see," like that was it. That is how you have to raise them—so they don't know anything.

My friend Sidney Byrd is at the table listening. She works for the Senders this year, but she was off Christmas week too, and didn't see this fight. She thinks the Senders are one family don't have enough to say to each other, so she is surprised there was carrying on over there. Husband and wife never speak, never argue. Sidney doesn't know Cheryl Ann well, because she's been away at the woman's college. I have seen her grow up. Mrs. Olive don't think much of her daughter. This has been true for years and years, I'd say since the child was ten. Sidney has noticed it the short time she's been there.

Of Lily's gossip, Sidney says, "I think Cheryl seems all right, but some will surprise you. No telling what hell the girl might raise."

"Sidney," I say, to tell her not to say *hell*, for the child, Lily, is just eleven. Her mother don't want her to curse and I don't believe in it. I have been watching Lily since she was born—took her home from the hospital 'cause her mamma wanted to sleep off the labor in the quiet.

Sidney tries to fix it, she says to Lily, "I'm not talking about *preacher* hell."

There, that word again. Sidney Byrd has been getting in trouble for what she says long as I have known her.

. . .

I have known her since I was sleeping three to the bed with my sisters in my daddy's house when he was a sharecropper over near Clarksboro at the north of the county. We put up tobacco when we were girls and should have been going to the school. She likes to speak her mind but I love her.

Since she has been working at the Senders', every weekday

afternoon I call for her when I am finished with cleaning and supper, and ready to go home. I use a field-hand whoop that slides from low up to high. For town it sounds a little wild and we both know it, but we like it.

I have a late meal with her—piece of pork with greens, maybe corn bread, food I don't make for Lily's parents. We have our time out together, waiting for our ride.

The man I used to be married to, Miller Jones, is our ride. He has a big red Pontiac with a turquoise interior. He has been coming around lately.

The Starks are the only white family I ever worked for. Sidney has been working in town much longer. She has lost more than one job for gossip, some because her bosses are crazy, like Mrs. McKenzie who died in a fire. White people don't know how to act, is what she always says. She has studied it. They are Baptists and they have fine things and ought to know something, but they do not. We have an excuse, she says, we have white people, but white people don't have one. In the houses she has worked in—not trash, the good families—she says the white women are fools the way they run from the men. They can't breathe hardly in their girdles, much less make any headway. They like to get caught. She's seen rich women be tackled by their husbands and their clothes torn, tumbling like football boys, and smile during it. The men can do anything they want, anything, she says. And sometimes the women too. Whichever it is, one day you get caught in the middle.

I say it is not true, for it has never happened to me. I have never been caught in the middle. But it is getting ready to happen.

"You ever notice a white man won't take up with a woman who has any normal idea what is going on?" she asks me that night after we hear the gossip from Lily. We are riding in Miller's car.

I say: "White women can't think too good, because none of

them eat enough. They wouldn't know a meal if you put it under their chins." I start to laugh, and I turn to Sidney who is in the back. Sidney won't sit up front with me and Miller even though he has the room.

"I mean it, why you cut them slack?" Sidney asks.

I don't answer. I don't know. I was born a peaceful person, want everybody to get along. Which is what makes all this hard to explain, if you look at it as it goes along, not all at once.

We get to her place, a tiny pink house with a porch coming off, and trumpet vines all over, not blooming, but full and still green, which seems a miracle this late in the winter. She lives with her mamma since her boyfriend, Raoul, was shot at the Golden Parrot. He was with another woman at the time. She has not gotten over it. I say good night to her. And all Sidney says to Miller is, "You go in to work after this, don't you?" Not ever a thank you for the ride.

Miller mumbles at her. He has a mustache these days, and as always, the big head. He is after me to marry him again, and he knows how Sidney feels. She believes he will run all over me if I let him back into my life. The way he did before.

I tell Sidney he has half an hour before he has to leave for his shift. And she says to me, "You can get into something in half a hour, Pauline, you watch it."

She slams that Pontiac door. I have always let Sidney tell me what to do, some. She has always had more opinions than I have.

• • •

I have been with Miller two different times: once when I was sixteen for two years, and again when I was twenty-five, for three and a half. Now we are in our thirties and he says he has changed. In some ways he has.

The first time I ran off with him to get away from my daddy's house—I was the second-oldest girl and my mamma was almost

blind. Everything fell on me. We married quick, and lived in colored enlisted housing up at Fort Bragg. The apartment was cinder
block, which was the most solid house I had lived in up to then.
We had good times. But Miller made me sick and I didn't know. By
the time I saw the army doctor he just went in without asking and
took my nature. After that I was nearly too sad to breathe. I
wouldn't go when Miller got transferred to California, even after
my daddy told me I was his wife and I should follow. I didn't want
nothing to do with him, when I learned what he had done, how he
got what he gave me. So I left and decided to see my oldest sister,
Rose, who lived in Philadelphia on welfare with four daughters,
and worked besides. She had a huge apartment, nice, warm, with
big windows, but there were too many streets in Philadelphia and
too many strangers. I worked in a factory sewing life preservers,
and had to ride a whole lot of busses to work before the sun rose,
and I never knew for sure the bus drivers would take me where
they said they were taking me. I just didn't trust them, don't know
why. Besides my sister Rose had men friends and one of them
liked me and I was done with men then, so I left. Went home and
found work with the Starks. I liked Mrs. Stark at the start. She was
dark-haired and from the North, that is, Chicago, and she said she
would teach me what I didn't know about cooking for white people
and keeping a house. And she did, then she got pregnant with Lily
and handed the child over—like I was the one knew everything
about a baby, that because I was colored I would know. So I
learned. Lily was a fat one with long arms, a girl and with sweet
breath. I couldn't stand it almost, how pretty she was when she
came out, the chubby creases at her wrists. I wanted her all to
myself, and I like to have got her.

About that time I was set up at the Starks', Miller showed in his
Pontiac. Drove it home from California. He had money for a house

from the Veterans and he said he would be true. So I went and lived with him in a place with shingles, and brick. But then he was gambling and drinking and we lost it all, including the furniture I had bought on time with Mr. Stark's name on the notes. I had to divorce him good that time, to leave his debts. Mr. Stark told me. I made Miller go to the courthouse and we both signed the paper.

. . .

And now, years have passed, and Miller has sobered up, and paid back everybody, including Mr. Stark, and got a good job—shift cook at the hospital—and the Pontiac engine rebuilt, and seats recovered. He has started showing up every day to give me a ride home from the Starks'. I have been bringing Sidney along so he doesn't try anything. He knows Sidney doesn't like him, but he drives her to keep me happy.

Sidney wants me to hate him. It has always been hard for me to hate people up until this.

. . .

February and March, Mr. Sender is Sidney's only subject besides Miller. I wish she wouldn't keep on it, for Lily hears everything. So I say to mock her, "Sounds like you care for him."

"I am just saying," she says. "I don't care. You the one who cares."

I think, it is not a sin to care for a person. Even if they are white. But Sidney is stronger than I am, so I have always believed, and I don't cross her.

"What do the preacher say?" Sidney says, to apologize. "I have been to that well many times, and I know now by heart it is dry." She means white people will always let you down and down and down no matter how they may seem. She has not always had this opinion, but she had it for the last few years. I am not ready to believe this about all of them, and she knows it.

"Something wrong with him," she says. "Like he's sick or dying. He don't leave the house. I'm just wondering what it is."

I see Lily considering Mr. Sender. She has sympathy for people, in this she takes after me. She gets right in other people's lives and leaves her own out. I do that too, sometimes.

But Lily is white with brown hair, nothing like me at all. She has glasses, and her mouth is crooked, and she thinks her daddy won't look at her because she is ugly, and her mother says she shouldn't eat so much. Yet I do feed Lily like a human being: I won't starve her. Every way else, I raise her like they want me to. I don't tell her what men do, or what her period is going to be, because her mother don't want me to. Mrs. Stark is a businesslike woman, works all the day long, but she thinks Lily should be spared, should grow up and marry rich, never cry. To do this you have to stay ignorant, she believes.

Palm Sunday coming on, Lily starts going over there to see Mr. Sender. I don't like it. He's not doing well, not going to work.

Right before Easter he sends over a big ugly fluffy stuffed duck with Sidney. I think Lily is getting pretty old for a stuffed toy, but she thinks it is great, and she runs upstairs and gives it a ribbon of her own for round its neck. So I am alone at the table with Sidney, who has been riding me all afternoon about Miller. I don't like looking at everything the way Sidney does. It makes me distrustful, and agitated.

Then Miller comes.

"Ready to go?" he asks at the back screen door, same as he always asks. He's on time, four-thirty. He's been on time for six months.

And something gets into me. I say to him, "Will you wait till I am done cooking? The corn pudding has not set."

He stands there a minute with his hat in his hand. He is

balding some and his eyes are dark and large. He says, softly, "If you say." And he sits on the back stoop and waits for us, like that.

When I have closed the back door on him, Sidney says, "Well, I didn't think I would live to see that."

I say, "See? He's changed, like he says he has." I am more amazed than Sidney. And I don't even feel terrible about it. I feel pretty good. That is the first mystery in this story.

"Just wait," Sidney says.

. . .

When I get home that night my sister Rose calls long distance from Philadelphia to tell me she is having another baby and she don't want it and she has prayed on it. She wants to go to a man in Allentown to get rid of it. She could possibly die if she goes to Allentown, but still she wants to do it. Her boyfriend doesn't know, and he wants to live with her, and four children is enough. If he lives with her and they find out, the new baby won't add, she won't get as big a check. But he is a mason and he has work, and he wants her, even if she doesn't get the check. She doesn't want to mess this up. He wants to marry her, even. So what should she do?

"Well, tell him, and ask him is he a man," I say to her.

She says would I say that. I say maybe, and this seems true, although I never asked it of Miller, I think now I might.

"You, Pauline?" she says. "*You?*"

. . .

A few days later Lily says Mr. Sender had her in to see him again, and I tell her right out she had better not go over there. He has guns in his den and he is out of his head, can't even get washed and dressed and go to work.

Lily for the first time gets that look other older white people get, and she says, "I don't have to listen to you."

There is no way around what she means.

Then she runs upstairs and she's crying.

Sidney says, "See? She just like the rest. Why you spoil her? See? Look at it, Pauline. And why can't she give her own self a ponytail, you still combing out her hair? And why can't she clean her room, or put her clothes in the hamper, or run her own bath?"

It breaks my heart how Lily spoke to me. And then I think, it's not right, the way she can speak to me. Say anything she wants.

. . .

A few days after, I am out in the garden hanging wash. I come in the house to see her, but the child doesn't answer. I remember that Sidney has left early for a funeral. I go over to the Senders', and stand on the back porch. There is a door split in the middle, and a window on top. I can see in—the back hall that goes to his den is unlit. Mrs. Olive's car is not in the driveway. I wonder if Sidney has locked up. I reach for the doorknob, then catch myself. My heart hurts in my chest.

Then I see Lily turn in the drive on her bicycle, so I settle down. She's sweet to me. She's sorry what she said the other day. I don't believe she is a bad child. I still don't believe that. But she is not my child.

That Friday Sidney tells me Mr. Sender is not even coming out to eat anymore. She says she doesn't think he wants to live.

. . .

That next Saturday in the A&P, I feel as if I've left the Starks' house with a pot going. I haven't even been there that day. I go shopping for the Starks before I go to work. I have the manager call for me, and I am waiting outside for one of the four cabs in Fayton what will haul colored people. I have hoped to get Sol Bascomb, who is one of my favorite white men. He has helped me from time to time, with my sweet potato pie business at Christmas, delivering.

It is Abel Odom who finally shows. A good old boy, the worst. Saggy face like a hound dog. I ask him can we hurry. He says he will see about that. There is something wrong with the latch on the trunk in his nasty cab, so he puts the Starks' groceries in the back. There is no room on the seat for me when he is through. I am too wide. I hesitate.

"What?" he says.

Sol and the other taxi drivers let me sit in front. I reach for the front door handle.

"What makes you think you can ride there?" he says.

So I get in the back, squeezed against seven brown bags of groceries. He slams the door before I'm all the way in, so my face jams up against the celery stalk poking out of one. The door handle is pressing in my back. He is going slow as he can down Sycamore Street. I am not going to be provoked, I tell myself. I am not, and on an ordinary day, I wouldn't be, but today I can hardly bear it. I am burning. I stare out the opposite window, over the seven standing bags of food. I see the white bungalows with waxy-leaved bushes in the yards, look like they never grow or change. These neighborhoods are hunched under the gray clouds. A house is never a color in this part of town, just brick or ghostly. All of Fayton is hunkered down. Finally, we pull into the Starks' drive.

Closer I get to the kitchen door, the worse I feel. Inside, I say, "Lily? You up?"

Odom is bringing in the bags because he knows I will tell Mrs. Stark if he doesn't. When he's finished I leave the tip on the table and go into Lily's bedroom. Nobody in the bed, nobody in the yard when I look out her window.

Soon as he's gone I run out of the Starks' house, across the side yard, and through the Senders' back gate.

I get to their back stoop. Dutch door is closed. I take the knob this time. Then I am standing in the back hall calling Lily's name. I see Mr. Sender's den door is closed.

I am strong in my body at this point in my life. I have put up tobacco and slaughtered stock, from the time I was eight until I left home with Miller. But it is the second mystery here, how I march down the Senders' hall without being invited in, and how I push in Mr. Sender's door, don't think about it.

He stands and Lily rolls out of his lap. Her shorts down around her little thighs, she tumbles to the floor.

I look at him straight in the face. I have never done this to a white man. This is the third: I see something gleamy-glinting dart behind his eyes, trying one eye, and then the other, as if his eyes are lookouts, and if it is quick enough, I won't be able to look in. I am held there in a stare. Lily is struggling with her pants. They are little cotton pique I put in bleach water and washed the day before. I yell at her to get out, but she can't walk yet, her legs are bound by the elastic.

That's when Mr. Sender reaches down for his long gun. Old, like the one my daddy borrowed once for close range, not for hunting. To kill a pig who had eaten what they had put in the barn for the rats. He wants to know what I think I'm doing in his house.

You know what he calls me.

He is looking right at me, with that pistol pointing in the air, the butt of it in the crook of his elbow jammed into his side. So I can't look down. Finally Lily crawls to my leg. I reach down one hand and yank up her shorts. I tell her to get out again, and she does it. I am still staring at Mr. Sender.

I see it again behind his eyes. It is trying to cram itself down into some lie, I see that.

When Lily is gone, it comes all the way out. And it is going to spit in my face, and then beat me good, and say how sorry it is. It is going to grab hold of me, and then to throw me down. I see it swirling around everywhere, not only in this time and in this room, but about Lily and me when we are alone, in the lies I have to tell her, the lies I have to go along with. I see what she can say to me. I see Miller when he's been cruel. I see that army doctor took what wasn't his to take. I see Odom when he slammed that car door on me, just ten minutes before.

I see it spread out over the whole of Fayton, and the people having to crawl low down, afraid to pull up for fear of it. It is stealing everyone's sight. It is the same as Mr. Sender's pipe smoke but it don't let up, it is drifting dark, making it hard to see or breathe, or to want to.

Then I see Mr. Sender there. He's in front of these other things I see. Yet I see them all. He is the gate to them, his open mouth is the door. He's calling me things, saying filthy things. There's his gun, but he looks too pitiful to be able to shoot me. It is pointed up, towards himself. I reach for his fingers holding that pistol. My hand covers his hand. I cannot believe what I am about to do.

Later in the day, Sidney says she is so shocked: "I thought some were bad but I wasn't ready for this white man. I revise my opinion, Mr. Sender takes the prize." Sent in there to clean up the blood, Sidney has read the notes he wrote that say, *I love Cheryl more than my whole life.*

"Been crawling in his daughter's bed since she was nine," Sidney says. "Imagine that. He confessed it on paper. I'd kill myself too if I was a wretch like that. Mrs. Sender don't think I can read? Been mulling over it holed up in that room, brokenhearted over his baby daughter taking a new lover. Call him her *new* lover. Can you imagine?"

And I lie to her and I say I can't.

For I don't say what I have done. Or anything about Lily. After, I have picked up Lily's flip-flops from the yard, and I have told Lily nothing happened, because that is my job and now I despise it. Lily has gone fast fast fast asleep. She's good at it. She's been raised to it.

By that night I know I must live another life. On that Monday I stop working for the Starks. I have been caught in the middle. I have been party to too much that is false.

. . .

Very late in my life, when I am about to die, I tell Miller the truth, because it doesn't seem right to pass on with it, take it with me where I am going. I still doubt myself sometimes, I still wonder then. He says, "You, Pauline? You a saint. *You?*" He refuses to believe me.

And I still cannot explain how it happened. How I knew. How I went through those two doors without fear. How I faced him, a white man holding a real pistol, mouth wide open, gaping gate to all those lies.

And I can't explain what happens right after: it comes to me to boss my sister Rose, that very night, tell her she better have that baby, and in a few months I go to Philadelphia on a bus and am not afraid of the driver. I am there when she is born and I name her Tamara. I bring her home from Philadelphia and I decide I will not stunt her, I will raise her right. I move in with Miller, and this time he does respect me because I make him. And we have Tamara for our child. He becomes a different man. Even Sidney admits it finally. The best part of my life happens after that day in Mr. Sender's den.

That Saturday, though, I can't know any of what will happen. In fact, I have no thought of the future, for if I do, I will surely run for my life. For the future I have just described cannot be imagined. I am just staring into his ugly eyes watching something I've never seen so clear dart here and there, trying to hide in some claim he is about to make. It is amazing to behold, brazen, dark. I know more words and more words are going to come out of his big brown pink mouth where the barrel will fit so perfectly, I see. I know what he will say: that the whole world is his, how that will never change. But he only owns one mean little part of the world, it is his lie that the smallest part is the whole, is everything. I must already know there is more that day when I reach up toward his arm, and pull down a little and squeeze his hand on the trigger, so the bullet goes through the roof of his mouth and into his brain. I just can't stand to hear him anymore, hear him tell his small mean lies over and over and over as if nothing can ever change.

The Odd Fellow

Tim Carter

It was the first day at Fayton High in 1964. The dark-eyed boy in homeroom seemed to know him. "You the one Mrs. Sender took in? The orphan? What's that like?" he asked. "I always wondered."

Eventually, Tim told Bit Cobb all about the Clarksboro Home where he was raised. The children had to wear white shirts to public school, so they were marked, called "the odd fellows." The Odd Fellows were like the Elks, just ran the place, but people over in Clarksboro could never remember that. Bit, who was really Benedict, told him he knew the difference between Odd Fellows and orphans. Then he wanted to know if Tim was going out for J.V.

Tim said yes to Bit because he liked him. He didn't know what sort of family he came from.

. . .

After practice a week later, a burgundy Cadillac drove up and stopped for the two of them. A beautiful brunette was driving. Bit called her Mamma. Tim said she looked too young to be that, and Bit said, "Everybody thinks so, but her most of all."

She seemed to know Tim's widowed aunt, Olive Sender, whom he was living with now. After asking after her, she suggested Tim come for a swim.

Tim thought they meant the Y, but Bit said, "My house," as they turned into Cobblee Acres, named for Bit's father who had built the entire subdivision.

Soon Tim was wandering in Bit's huge yellow brick colonial. He'd never seen such a house. There was a color TV and the refrigerator made ice. Bit came out in regular canvas trunks. He gave Tim an electric blue swimsuit that hardly covered his parts. His mother had bought it—Bit said he hated it, but it was his only spare. Tim tried to be grateful, although he did feel naked out by the pool. He thought Bit's mother would make some joke, for he was as white as a flour biscuit, but she said, "Look at his feet."

They used to call them hooves at the home. His arches were so high shoes hardly fit. But Mrs. Cobb called them "beautiful."

Nobody had ever called anything on him beautiful before. His head, he knew, was wide. His eyes were very pale green.

Bit's chubby little sister, Dora, was there. His daddy, a big man with a mustache, called Tulip, showed at six. When Mrs. Cobb pointed out Tim's feet, Mr. Cobb's answer was to show his own, flat as flippers, and say, "Army sent me home over these."

"He wanted to be an officer, think of that," Mrs. Cobb said, as if it were a joke, slapping her husband's wide thigh, so it turned bright red. Tim wondered why she'd do that in front of him.

Mr. Cobb said to Bit, "Come here, son."

Bit dragged himself over, the picture of reluctance. Tim was surprised.

"How was practice?"

Bit said he got cramps running twenty laps. Then his father punched him in the stomach right where he said it hurt—it was a roughhousing punch, friendly, Tim thought. "Coach going to teach you something?"

Tim saw Bit should answer, but Bit didn't see it.

Mr. Cobb said, "Say, *Yes Sir.*"

Bit answered, and then ran and jumped in the pool, coming up to Tim to whisper, "You smoke?" and Tim said, "Of course."

"Let's get out of here," Bit said.

"Now?" Tim asked—he'd just gotten used to the blue-green water, its silkiness. He'd never had a pool almost to himself before.

• • •

Tim was happy enough once he'd put his pants back on, and was walking. The subdivision was a wonderland. The houses were brick—not sorry wood the way they were in Clarksboro. Some had steep roofs, others, high porches with columns. Bit asked more questions about Tim's life in that tobacco town. Tim described bright-leaf auction time, when the nicotine in the air made your brain feel sweet and stocked up. He told Bit about the boys at the home who wailed at night, about the dirty walls, the baby collie he sneaked home once, that ended up suffocating under his bed. Tim left some parts out—he didn't think Bit would understand what it was like to live your life knowing it was all borrowed, or second-hand, like the half-busted toys or the clothes he would get in the home for Christmas. They all denied the gifts were used, even showed him the store tags on occasion, but Tim knew better. How could Bit see that, when everything new and bright obviously fell right into his hands? He didn't even have to take the trouble to want.

When Tim was dropped off back at Aunt Olive's that night, he almost hoped he wouldn't see Bit again. Bit's life was so easy and plentiful Tim couldn't help but covet, which was a painful thing.

• • •

Bit didn't make the coach's last cut until his daddy put in a dona-tion to the uniform fund. The coach was delighted with Tim—his hooves could kick, as it turned out.

Bit's parents were always up in the stands, cheering. Aunt Olive came once but the bleachers made her stiff, so she didn't come again.

Tim realized early that Aunt Olive had no talent for raising a boy. She had brought up one girl, Cheryl Ann, that people called crazy—she left home soon after her daddy died, and barely wrote. Aunt Olive put Tim in her daughter's room, but didn't take the lace curtains down. She couldn't seem to understand how much a boy could eat, that he had to shave. Around her Tim always felt that he should shrink, or wash. He didn't complain, though, for then he'd be looking at Clarksboro.

Bit hardly played that first season, just the nonconference game against the team the county high put up. The one chance he got, he fumbled. Tim insisted they practice. Bit was catching passes pretty well in the driveway one day in December, but he quit as soon as his daddy walked up. Tim threw the football to Mr. Cobb, who caught it, saying, "Why don't you pass like Tim, Bit? What's so hard?" Tim saw the comparison hurt Bit. He didn't want to feel good about it, but he still did.

. . .

Bit proposed they camp out the next night. He was pretending they were "running away"—he packed a great many provisions. Going in, they heard barking. In Clarksboro some boys trained their mongrels on the orphans, so Tim didn't like that. Bit told him that in the woods around Fayton there were dogs gone back to wild running in packs. These were bred but their masters left them behind if they didn't act right in the hunt, didn't point and grovel.

Tim said why would somebody throw out his own dogs he raised? Bit said Tim would be surprised. A mangy spaniel came up when they got in deep. The animal was shivering, and on his ears were throngs of ticks. Tim said he could see the dog missed men. Bit said, "Yeah? I think they figure it out."

It was a whole lot colder than it was supposed to be that night. They lit a big fire—Tim took out the marshmallows from Aunt Olive, who had as much as told Tim she liked the fact that he had a rich boy to visit. Wealthy as he was, Bit didn't have many friends. Tim was the only one Bit took home. The other boys Bit hung around with were too tough to meet Mrs. Cobb, Tim figured.

After a while, Bit pulled out three Ball jars of corn liquor he had lifted from under the stairs at the Elks Club, where they stashed what the sheriff's boys got from stills before Christmas. He said he broke a window to get them. Tim thought, why should somebody with everything steal, but he felt it was wrong to say it.

Halfway through the first jar Tim threw up. Bit didn't mock him—he was grateful for this. Then Bit started playing the harmonica, and after a while, he was talking to the stars, asking them why they glowed. Then he passed out on the bare ground. It was going into the teens. Tim covered him.

At two a.m., Tim was too cold even inside the tent. He was going back to the house. His breath was huge clouds out in the open, but he couldn't see Bit's at all. He couldn't wake him. He hooked his arms under Bit's and dragged him all the way back to the patio, almost half a mile.

Mr. Cobb came out and screamed at his son, limp in Tim's arms, "Where in hell did you get the liquor?"

Mrs. Cobb showed up, shouting, and saved Tim from having to tattle. They spent the rest of the night in the hospital.

Alcohol makes it easier to freeze to death, they were told. Bit came close, but they brought him around. In the morning Bit's mother came up to Tim and put her hands on his cheeks. He thought how pretty she was, how soft her voice—he could not ignore it. She planted a kiss close to his mouth, and said, "You know you are my kind of boy? You know you are a hero?"

He had never felt before what it was to shine in front of a beautiful mother.

When Tim went in to see him, Bit asked, "Remember things were glowing? I was kicking it. Somebody came in here, asked me if I was trying. A counselor. What else did I say? You think I was trying?"

"Trying what?" Tim asked.

"Don't you get it?" Bit asked, then paused. "You don't. Maybe that's what I like about you."

"What?"

"You don't see through it at all, you just see the outside."

At that point, Tim didn't know what Bit could possibly mean by "it." It was a long time before he would.

. . .

In spring Bit's mother started calling Tim to invite him over on Saturdays. As a way to say thank you, she said, "for dragging the boy back to us."

When Tim got there sometimes, Bit would still be in bed. It felt odd to be talking to Bit's mother alone, but he loved doing it, usually, that was the truth. They sat at the kitchen counter eating the eggs she cooked. She'd show Tim pictures of Bit when he was little, and say, "He was such a good boy back then." Then she started telling Tim her high school stories. Later, she described how she had designed that fancy house, told him where she found the antiques.

Tim believed everything was fine between him and Bit, or just about. Then one day, by the pool, Bit said to him, "Did my mother say she had me when she was a child?"

Tim said she did.

"Did she tell you she was disappointed about life?"

Tim said she had hinted it, but he didn't think it meant much.

Bit got closer, and said, "She tell you Daddy took her out when she was vulnerable right after she lost homecoming queen? She say Daddy was only on the football team so they could list his two-hundred-some pounds in the program? She say it took her years to get him to start making real money because he was too bound to his mamma?"

She had said some of these things, but Tim didn't know what to do with them. He said, "Maybe."

"She mention," he went on, "that he was so heavy the first time she couldn't breathe during or sit down after?"

Tim hated the way Bit had said these things out loud. Some stories should stay quiet—he thought Bit ought to know that. Bit said, "She look at you like this?" Then he made his mother's face when her black eyes went slanted and shiny. His lips trembled exactly the way hers did. Tim fixed on the beauty of Bit's mouth, so like his mother's mouth, but it scared him when he did that. Bit said, mocking his mother's voice, *"Isn't it just terrible?"*

Tim said, "Well, maybe it is," and then he pushed Bit in the water.

They fought briefly, Bit held Tim down—Tim thought maybe he had the right to, for a minute. But when he needed his breath, he shoved Bit out of the way. It was so easy to do that. Too easy, he thought later.

. . .

That August, on the first day of football practice, Tim saw Mr. Cobb slap Bit right in front of the field house, and wondered what

Bit had done to deserve it. Bit staggered into the locker room, trying not to cry. The other boys thought he was soft: Tim stood with
Bit. He helped him outside, and Bit went ahead and let it out,
pushing Tim away so he could be alone. He wept on the sidewalk,
like someone pitiful, Tim thought. He really wanted to leave Bit
there, but he didn't do it.

In Spanish class in September, Bit told Tim his daddy had
stopped talking to him completely because he wouldn't go back to
football. Tim told Bit he should keep trying, and Bit said, "I don't
know why I tell you anything."

"I'm your friend," Tim said.

Bit glared at him.

. . .

Tim was first string the next year and he joined the alpaca
sweater crowd, the ones who like to be believed rich, called the
"grits." They strolled through the high school halls in twenty-dol-
lar wing tips and starched shirts. Tim couldn't help but think, this
is me, Tim Carter from the Clarksboro Odd Fellows Home—pass-
ing. This was when the high school was still the center of the uni-
verse in Fayton, the second-to-last year it was all white.

It was hard to dress right with no money. He had to get a job at
the Piggly Wiggly to pay for the clothes. He had to learn to iron
and use starch, for Aunt Olive said she couldn't afford the laundry.
At parties, he danced to Otis Redding with girls in hose and wool
sweaters and matching skirts. They wore girdles. Their hips felt
like wood.

Bit joined in with the ones who wore their hair too long. Every
four weeks or so, his daddy forced him to the barber, and he'd
show up with a crewcut people made fun of. Even Tim did, a little.

In November, Bit took Mrs. Cobb's Cadillac and wrecked it. He
stayed over at his girlfriend Nyla's house Thursday before home-

coming, and showed up at second period in his clothes from the day before. The whole grade knew the story by lunchtime. He was a sensation—a real bad boy.

. . .

A few weeks later there was a rumor that Nyla was pregnant. It was also going around that Mr. Cobb had thrown Bit off the porch, but Tim didn't believe either thing. Then he heard Bit had run away. That, he believed, crazy as it was.

The last day before the Christmas holidays, Dora revealed to Tim that Bit had called the house one night. She said, "I told— they traced the call to Myrtle Beach. You think I shouldn't have?"

Tim said Bit was a runaway. "We've got to settle him down," then he thought, why did he say "we"—Bit wasn't his job.

"He was tripping, he told me so," Dora said, and she stopped. "You won't tell, will you?"

. . .

On Christmas Eve that year Mr. Cobb drove up to Aunt Olive's house in a big square peculiar-looking car, and came to the door to say, "We were wondering if you could help. My wife is beside herself." Aunt Olive told Tim to go.

But Mr. Cobb wasn't in a hurry. They headed off down Winter toward Locust, and then turned into one of the poorest parts of town that still had white people in it, where all the houses were one-story and wood, near the closed cotton mill. A few had big plastic candy canes in the yards, and colored lights on the porches. Mr. Cobb pointed to a shabby house on a corner, and said, "Isabel grew up there."

Tim found this surprising, because Mrs. Cobb had told him many times how she had married down. Soon they were on county roads, not heading to Cobblee. Mr. Cobb wanted to tell Tim things, have time alone with him. He started by describing how much he loved to watch Tim play football. He confessed he was an awful player. He could never run fast, never, even when he lost weight in the army. He had a brother named Archie who could run, but he died in his late twenties because he took dope from the hospital. He called his brother a fiend and he said Bit took after him. Tim told Mr. Cobb not to say that, and the big man gave him a fast, hard look, like a dagger, which disappeared as quickly as it had appeared. Then Mr. Cobb popped his jaw and picked up speed in the car, and called Tim "son." At the sound of it, "son," Tim pricked up like a hound dog. He felt this in himself, he couldn't stop it. Mr. Cobb reached over and put his arm way around Tim. "I'm going to tell you something else." Mr. Cobb's arm weighed on him and felt wonderful at the same time. Tim was bracing for more Cobb secrets—he didn't know what to do with them, and he had so many already. He was grateful when Mr. Cobb said: "This, Tim, is a Mercedes-Benz. First one in Fayton County. You are sitting on a pure leather seat. Feel it. First time? Make a wish."

• • •

Mrs. Cobb was with a sheriff's deputy on the settee by the huge tree in the parlor. The man was very young and he kept looking all around the room, at the Victorian furniture, the flocked wallpaper. Mrs. Cobb was smoothing the velvet on a pillow in her lap.

When Tim walked in the den he saw Dora had her feet up on the coffee table and this upset him—he knew how hard Mrs. Cobb had worked buying all her antiques, so he said something.

"What?" Dora asked him. "This isn't your house."

"I'm sorry," he said, knowing she was right. But he also knew something in him wasn't sorry.

He asked Dora questions, but she said, "I should never have told you anything. I'm the one Bit talks to, not you."

Then Mrs. Cobb came in and hugged him. "Oh Tim, you have to help."

When her mother left, Dora turned to Tim and said, "My brother would be mixing purple Jesus by now."

In the other room, Mrs. Cobb was going through the litany of the ways Bit had gone wrong since age ten, for the deputy. Tim was listening. Bit had never done anything right, not for years, according to his mother. He'd never heard her add it all up like that before.

"Well?" Dora said.

Tim wasn't going into the Cobbs' refrigerator. He wasn't grabbing anything he wasn't offered. People might take it wrong.

"What if somebody kidnapped him?" he said, sliding down to the other end of the couch, away from Dora.

"He was leaving Myrtle for another beach, nobody kidnapped him," she said. "You can ask Nyla. Mamma won't say her name. She's lying and making eyes at the deputy."

"She isn't flirting," Tim defended her.

"What do you call it?" Dora said.

· · ·

Mrs. Cobb called him into the hall to say, "We are going to that little whore's house. You are going to get what she knows. Then tell her you are certain we will pay for her to go to Rome and nothing else."

She meant the abortionist in Rome, Georgia, a real butcher, Tim had heard. He didn't say this, although he thought it—Mrs. Cobb was already so upset.

At quarter to eleven that night, he was standing in Nyla's doorway, and saying to her, "They love their boy, they want what is best for you." He knew some of this wasn't true.

Nyla was staring up at him, and she was sucking hard on a peppermint. "I am not knocked up it turns out, I am on the rag right now. Why don't you run tell her?"

He couldn't believe her mouth.

When she let him in, she said, "Don't you think it is creepy his parents go cheer at your games? Bit's off the team."

"Bit doesn't care," Tim said, which he didn't think was really true. But how could he help what the Cobbs did. How could he stop enjoying hearing Mr. Cobb boom, "TIM TIM TIM."

"You know what Bit said to me?" she asked.

Tim humored her.

"Every time they come into his room, he feels like they are looking for some other perfect boy, who is hiding maybe under the bed, in the closet. It is as if they have a searchlight. He stands right in front of it, the light shines through. His daddy is completely ashamed of him. His mamma—"

"He could try harder," Tim said.

"Don't you see all he does is try? But what do they want?"

Tim said, "They give him everything. He has everything."

"So do they," she said, "and look at them."

Tim didn't know what she meant by *Look at them.* "He just has to meet them halfway," Tim said. "Bit doesn't do right by them or you either—"

She softened and offered him a Pepsi, sat by him on the couch, and put her legs on the coffee table. She wasn't wearing any hose. He knew Bit's hand had been on Nyla's thigh. She wouldn't feel like wood. He could be feeling exactly what Bit felt. Then he caught himself. He was here for Mrs. Cobb. He had to lie to Nyla a little to get her to trust him. He didn't like that part. But the Cobbs had been good to him.

Eventually, he ran out to the car to tell what he'd heard. Mrs. Cobb's response was, "That cunt could have ruined us." He told himself Mrs. Cobb wasn't herself.

• • •

With Nyla's story, a private detective found Bit in an empty cottage at North Salter Island, dealing marijuana to beachcombers. A few days after Christmas Mr. Cobb sent his men down to the beach to pull his son out.

When they invited Tim over for New Year's night, he didn't want to go. Aunt Olive told him, "People don't say no to Tulip Cobb."

Soon as he walked in, Dora told him he was a traitor. Tim didn't think that was it, and he said so. He was happy to see Bit in front of the TV, eating his mother's Chex Mix. Bit was skinny, but okay. He wouldn't even look at Tim.

Finally Tim said, "They had to have you home."

Bit growled, "That's what you would do, what you did? Home? They are sending me away."

"Where?" Tim said. He was very surprised.

"Altamount Military in the Blue Ridge up near Asheville. For wayward boys. You think I'm wayward, Tim? Try this fucking house—I guess you have—" His dark eyes flashed like his mother's—Tim couldn't help but think of Bit's mother. Moles on his white skin. Bit started to stomp off.

"We aren't rude to our guests, Bit," Mr. Cobb said, pushing him back. "We don't use that language, you damn—"

Tim was sitting on the red leather La-Z-Boy, but hoping to leave. Mr. Cobb said to him, "You stay here, talk to him, tell him what an idiot he's been." It was uncomfortable, being put up against Bit, being favorably compared, being asked to give advice. He knew he shouldn't like it but something in him did.

After Bit went up to Altamount, Tim didn't see the Cobbs for months. It was an easier life, really, without them. They always made him feel as if he needed more than he had, that he could walk into that life. Since it was false, it felt uncomfortable. There was no reason to visit—Bit was out of the house, and Dora despised him. He resolved to spend more time with his aunt, but she talked all the time about how much everything cost. She fired her maid, Sidney. Tim had to show her how to use a vacuum cleaner, how to make dinner. He tried to pity her, get her to smile.

In March, when Mrs. Cobb invited him over for pork barbecue out of the blue, he was excited to go. As soon as he arrived, he went right for the kitchen, and heaped his plate. Dora's platter was piled up like his, but her mother took it away from her and dumped everything off except a tablespoon. "What is wrong with you?" she asked her. "You want to look like a Cobb?"

He kept going over there that spring. There was something odd about it, with Bit not there, but he couldn't help himself, they were so generous. In late April they decided he should run for senior class treasurer. They stayed up late making the signs. Mrs. Cobb popped popcorn. When they got tired, they jumped in the pool, the three of them—Dora refused to join in.

One midnight right before the election, Mrs. Cobb said Tim should stay over. It was too late to drive him home.

"Sleep in Bit's room," she said.

The problem was, Tim loved Bit's room—the shag carpet, the plaid curtains, the shelves, the books on the shelves: *Huckleberry Finn, Catcher in the Rye, Twenty Thousand Leagues Under the Sea.* He was afraid to sleep in it, partly because he had always wanted to. When he slipped under the sheets, at first he felt as if he were stealing. But then he told himself he was just borrowing this bed, this boy's room, for a single night, and borrowing was something he'd been doing his whole life. Then he could fall asleep, and even dream.

In the morning, homemade pancakes, Mrs. Cobb in her pretty nightgown and her let-down hair—he kept thinking Bit would be walking in any minute, that he could hear him in the hall. It was good to get back to Aunt Olive's, in a way—nothing made him uneasy when he was there. But when he went back into the room he slept in, with the lace curtains, the old sagging shades, he thought back on Bit's—he couldn't help it.

The day he won class treasurer Mr. Cobb was outside the principal's office to congratulate him. He told Tim they were driving over to Keaneville where East Atlantic College was. Tim was hoping to go there on a football scholarship when he graduated. He was thinking Mr. Cobb was going to show him the campus. Instead, he pulled up in front of a store with the sign, "First Quarter. Haberdashers Since 1946." "Get you some good clothes, boy," he said. "You will be a big man on campus next year."

When Tim was in the dressing room, trying on cashmere for the first time ever, he heard Mr. Cobb announce to the salesman, "My boy is thinking of the Citadel."

Tim ran out, and said, "Altamount turn Bit around?"

"Not Bit," Mr. Cobb said, "you. You have it in you, don't you? First time I saw you, I knew."

He'd never thought of a military academy. He knew they hazed you, tore you down, he knew what that was from Clarksboro. "What's wrong? You don't like the outfits? How we got you elected? What?"

Tim didn't know how to answer. Of course he liked the outfits. Of course he was grateful.

"Speechless?" Mr. Cobb punched him the way he did Bit sometimes. He'd never done that before. It hurt.

. . .

When they pulled into the carport later, Tim was thinking of making an excuse and not staying for dinner. He didn't know why really, he just needed to be back at Aunt Olive's, be in his own surroundings. But Mrs. Cobb came out to yell, "Altamount found a hash pipe on him. He's getting expelled." She practically begged Tim to stay.

That night, they talked in front of Tim, as if he were a member of the family. They decided to send Bit to a "wilderness experience" in Arizona. They were not letting him come home first, that would seem like a "reward," they decided. Didn't Tim think so? They spoke of Bit as a loss, a mistake, a thing, a big problem. Tim told himself they couldn't mean it—they were just at the end of their rope.

. . .

About a week later Tim heard from friends that the Cobbs were taking Dora to Europe to be "finished."

Summer, he worked full shifts at the Piggly Wiggly, and when he came home he'd have the egg salad sandwiches Aunt Olive thought were supper. The Cobbs were so far away. It seemed to him that they had fallen off the face of the earth. He was standoffish about the clothes Mr. Cobb had bought him, but towards the end of the summer, he started taking them out and trying them on. He'd catch himself in the mirror, see the boy he resembled— someone who took silk and cashmere for granted, who didn't have to borrow it, or work for it, or even ask for it. He let himself dream of being that boy, not just posing as him, or standing in for him. It didn't seem as if it would do any harm. He knew he'd never be that boy, after all.

But in a few minutes, he didn't know why, he'd start to feel a nerve-wracking buzz, like the static behind a game on the radio. Then he'd take the clothes off. It wasn't until he put them back and packed them in camphor, inside zippered bags, that the feeling completely went away.

. . .

September Dora showed up in a tiny new Karmann Ghia. He was happy to see her somehow, even though he didn't like her, and she certainly didn't like him. This was mysterious, but true. Her face was different. At her mother's suggestion, she'd had all her back teeth pulled in France to sink her cheeks. Her lipstick was white. Her nose was different, too—it turned up. She told him, "Say something."

Even though she looked bizarre, Tim said she looked beautiful. She asked him if he were mocking her.

Tim said certainly not.

"You hear?" she said.

"What?" he said.

"Bit ran off from that wilderness place. He called once and said they left him in the desert and told him to find his own way back. Orienteering. He ran, found a road and hitchhiked. He said those people in Arizona wouldn't care if he died."

"Where are they looking?" Tim said.

"He said he's eighteen soon and he's not going to fight in the war, he's not being drafted, he is going incognito. Daddy says he doesn't care what he does now."

"Don't you know he does care?" Tim said.

She looked at him with eyes of metal, as if he were absurd. Finally, she said, "Come on, get in the car. You have to. They will come if I don't bring you. But you listen—from now on you aren't getting away with anything."

When he thought of this afternoon years later, he could remember that when he heard Dora's threat, he sensed a kind of gravity, pulling him back to the curb. He heard another voice, *It's the Cobbs, they are always so nice to you, anxious to see you, move*—that was the old one, but he was hearing a new one as well.

Both Mr. and Mrs. Cobb opened the door when he got there. Cold was blasting out. They had the air on high so they could show off their new English sweaters.

On the counter back in the kitchen, everything Tim loved to eat—greens, hush puppies, sweet potatoes, pork. Mr. Cobb mentioned that Tim's aunt was thinking of moving into an apartment, one he owned. Tim knew nothing of this.

"So how would you feel about moving in with us?" Mrs. Cobb asked.

"When we make this formal, we can go ahead. Try to get you an appointment. People know us." Mr. Cobb added.

Tim asked what they meant by "formal."

"We adopt you. You are still seventeen. The Citadel," Mr. Cobb said. "You surprised?"

Dora said, meekly—you could hardly hear her—"I have a brother."

Mrs. Cobb said, "How does this concern you? You just coast through, eat like a horse." It wasn't true. Dora must have weighed ninety-five pounds at that point. Mrs. Cobb turned to Tim. "Do you know how I have devoted myself to her appearance? And look at her." Then she paused. "Well, what do you say?"

He did not answer. He thought, "What about Bit? Bit?" He heard that deep tone getting louder. He was trying to make out what it was saying. Mrs. Cobb started to look very strange to him, as if her face were breaking into pieces. He had dreamed of this, of being their son, someone's—he knew that. But not this exactly—he saw the differences between what he had imagined, and this particular afternoon with the Cobbs. He looked at their white-mouthed child with the bony knees and the two of them wearing Shetland wool in August. They seemed to have gotten larger, suddenly too close. The chilled, sweet air pressed down on him too, as did the scent of the food, the smoothness of the leather lounger by his leg—there was nothing between him and these things now, no fence, no glass, no "as if." He felt unprotected. Things were so close they were breaking apart.

Mr. Cobb turned to Tim with a drink in his hand, and said,

"Don't you know what to say? Thank you? To Isabel here, thank you. What is your problem, son?"

"Stop it," she said, "let him think."

Tim discovered, sometime after he had done it, that he had opened the sliding glass doors, and walked out past the pool. He did not become fully aware that he had left them until he was jumping the fence, for his pants leg tore. He kept running, lighting out for those woods. He went through acres, heard the dogs. At the creek, where he'd camped with Bit that time he saved him, he stumbled, and stopped. He told himself he was only going to rest for a moment.

· · ·

Mrs. Cobb had a flashlight. She came upon him, folded over at the bank. She crouched beside him—"Don't let my husband set you off. He disgusts me. And Bit, there has always been something wrong with him—we know that. But you are going to turn out so well. Don't you see that? We see that. What is it?"

It was very clear, it came through then: he should hunker down there, near the earth, it would hold him. Keep his head low. When it was safe, get up and start walking. Away. He said in a low, new voice, "Don't ask for me, Mrs. Cobb, please don't ask, please. You have a son, Bit's your son."

"Not anymore is he my son. What will he turn out to be?—"

In that moment, Tim was shown the ways he'd disappoint them. He had already started disappointing them—running out here like this, not saying "yes sir," not knowing how to be grateful. He wasn't a soldier, or even a cadet. He was only so tough, not really tough. For the first time since he'd known the Cobbs, he was completely clear about them. No, his heart said, no. But then, a part of him insisted he look at that beautiful house and the pool lights through the scrub trees. From this distance it was all gleaming again, and whole. Mrs. Cobb was saying, "Come on back. You are my kind of boy."

He shivered. He was starting to feel sick, and weak—and already angry at himself, defeated. Perhaps if it had been daylight, in the open, not in those woods with those mangy hounds barking—

She said, "You are my son now." And a shudder went through him. For years he despised his weakness, that he didn't run, or stand his ground.

When she bent down to kiss him before she took him back, he shirked away to avoid her lips, the way Bit always used to.

It

Claire McKenzie, 1973

The place was decent-sized, and very new. The reception area had magazines for women, the ones about clothes and houses. There was a blue carpet, and we were high up for a suburban building, on the fourth or fifth floor. We were north of the city, in White Plains. There was little noise inside or outside, except the highway down below, which roared.

Tim, who looked miserable, took a seat catercornered from me. He'd driven all night to be here. He didn't want to face me. His presence was a compromise, a temporary accommodation as far as I was concerned. I had been told somebody had to come with me. He said yes because he had some notion of being a gentleman, I thought.

We were here to correct an error I didn't blame Tim for, even though he may have blamed himself. I never considered it his fault. I was just beginning to blame Appleton, a man whose love I had actually wanted, but not in the ordinary sense.

The first thing Tim said that morning that wasn't purely necessary was, "Do you want a drink?" I nodded, watched him walk over to the cooler and return, hugging the tiny cone of a cup. He had big nails, thick tips. There was so much energy implied in those hands, those arms, those high-arched feet—not actual, just implied, I thought. From the start, I'd decided that nothing about Tim was very realized. It wasn't his fault. He'd had a terrible life.

They called my name, Claire McKenzie. A nurse appeared and took me down a hall. She told me that soon, we'd have our interview, but that wasn't true. For a long time I had to sit in a waiting room and try not to think. It was cold in there, frigid. Of course everything rushed up.

. . .

I'd run into Tim on the campus back in June, on the same day I'd started Arnold Appleton's graduate painting seminar. I'd come down from my college in Virginia just to take the class. I had finished that spring, but hadn't decided where to go to graduate school. I was sort of shopping for a good teacher. Appleton was a very important painter, I thought. I'd shown him my picture of a family of figures set out in front of a wide, white landscape. I was very proud of it. Appleton had said it might be okay if the folks in the picture weren't dead. I was devastated. But then I told myself he was a real artist. Blunt. Cruel. Not wishy-washy like my teachers in Virginia. Besides, if Appleton didn't think I could really paint, then what? I had made up my mind early what I was going to do. I felt I had to justify myself, I had to prove myself. I believed something like this: if I wasn't an artist, basically, I had no right to live, or be happy. I thought I had my reasons. I had my reasons, but they weren't what I thought they were.

I was leaving the art building, about to cry, fiercely fighting it, and there was Tim, sauntering toward the library. A man from another world. From Fayton. I waved, and so did he, for we sort of knew each other. We came from the same hometown—he'd moved there the year I went away to boarding school. He'd lived with his aunt Olive Sender, my neighbor, then got mixed up with Bit Cobb's family. Bit had run to Europe to get out of the draft about the same time. I'd heard Tim had been adopted, but it hadn't turned out well.

He said he was in school the summer session because he had to pass a certain English course before he could be in the upper division. You had to write a ten-page paper. He'd flunked twice. He had to get out of this place—it was like limbo, he said. He felt as if he were behind—he had been at the Citadel for a semester, which had been a disaster, then he came to the university, but stopped after sophomore year, did a tour in Vietnam. That was the last thing he'd done on Tulip Cobb's say-so. He had cut it off with those people. He was alone in the world, except for his aunt. He was too old for these students, he said, he'd seen too much. He was working his way through. He was a carpenter.

A big university seemed like heaven to me, compared to my girls' school up in Virginia—a place where southern daddies of a certain class liked to store their daughters until further notice, i.e., marriage. I was out of place there. I was extremely ambitious; I had no plan of marrying. Secretly, I didn't think anyone would ask.

An idea came to me. I said I'd help Tim with his paper if he would do me a huge favor. I needed a model. I didn't tell him he'd be perfect because he was so odd—a vet, and rough, and not like other people I knew, anybody like me knew, or even wanted to know. He said it was a deal.

I believed I needed a neurasthenic, thoughtful man, if I needed a man at all. I had a crush on a first-year graduate student in my class, Peter, with a reddish, pointed beard and a ponytail. He liked to talk about the revolution. Peter was romantic to me; Tim was a hick.

I'd never had the experience of being alone with a model before, of being the one to tell the model what to do with his arms, his chin, his knees. The teacher—all my painting teachers had been men—had generally done that. The models were women nine times out of ten. Tim let me pose him. I worked fast, "alla prima," the way Appleton showed us. Oil and oil crayon on canvas, no underpainting. I sketched Tim's big square head. Ultramarine, sienna, burnt umber. Fast, big brushes. The whole experience was very private, very freeing. I started about seven. When I looked up at the clock, it was ten.

Appleton asked me where I found the caged animal. But he wasn't as cruel at that critique as he'd been the week before. He was expansive that day. He said an artist's job is to go to the sources of the things, the bare beating beginnings, and bring them into the world for people to see. It is a ruthless job, he said. "And of course, yes, it is a sacrifice." That's how he said it, "Yes, of course, a sacrifice." As if he knew very well what the word meant. As if he were very used to the idea.

I coaxed Tim over to my tight little studio on the north end of campus again that night, offered to pay him, but he refused. I drew him. I thought of him as pretty, and odd. There was a tough-ness, he'd been an orphan. "But you are an orphan too," he told me, "you and your sister, Sweetie." He knew my sister a little, back home. He talked about the two of us. Sweetie and I were mother-less, we had that in common, but nothing else. She was eight years younger, and ferociously conventional, head cheerleader, that sort of girl. I was another kind of ferocious. Perhaps if we'd had a mother, we'd have had some moderation, we wouldn't have been so extreme, so different. He seemed to understand all this, which surprised me. I rarely talked about what I was missing. Eventually, I changed the subject.

Those first few nights, I smoked cigarettes while I sketched

him, and sometimes ate a Baby Ruth or two. When I was exhausted, we parted ways. I trucked across campus to my girl dorm
where a student named Babette sat at the desk to monitor comings
and goings. Twice in one week, I arrived five minutes before curfew.

The next Monday Appleton came over after class to tell me the
sketches of Tim were "going in the right direction." I rejoiced.

That night Tim didn't show. I sat in that little studio and fumed,
then went looking for him the next day. He was living with a
widow who gave him a room for doing small jobs, the way he had
before, with old Mrs. Sender. I'd never been to this place, but the
house wasn't hard to find—it was the oldest building on the block,
a shabby bungalow, stuck in between two fraternity houses.

I saw him walking on the widow's driveway holding a tire. His
hair was mousy brown but that morning it caught the sun. His
eyes were mint green—they didn't seem real. I suddenly asked
myself what all those busts and heads of him were about. No wonder Appleton said he was caged—I hadn't given him enough
room. I'd have to do his whole body. I knew all this in a place
around my ribs as much as in my head.

He was in such a good mood I forgot to reproach him. He said
he liked a plate joint on an alley where they gave you two sides and
meat plus all the biscuits you could swallow. He'd buy.

My thought was, such country food, unsophisticated. But I was
trying to get him back—only because he was my key to pleasing
Appleton, I thought.

It was a low, small place and a black woman in the back who
owned it called out to you when you came in and told you where to
sit. It dated back to when the university was only for boys—there
were no salads on the menu, and the portions were enormous.

Tim apologized, said he'd left a message for me with Babette.

All night, he'd worked on his paper. Just that morning the teacher had told him his draft was probably going to work. He was wildly happy. I found him quaint.

I said I'd eaten, but it wasn't true. I just couldn't eat. It had come to me like a commandment, about the same time I'd seen him at the widow's house. In fact, everything else that happened that summer followed from that hour, when I saw him in the widow's driveway, and followed him to this low-lying plate place, with dreams of how Appleton would praise me.

He ordered the Salisbury steak, and greens, and sweet tea, while he spoke about the wonders of index cards and outlines. I had solved a mystery for him.

It wasn't that it didn't look good, in a certain way, the food. I'd been raised on greens with pot liquor, corn bread, peas with black eyes. I was from a humble little town, where that was what people ate. So was he. But I had to get back to the studio. I offered to pay him to continue to be my model.

"Why? I like watching you. You are so single-minded. You always know what you think, too. It's a gift—" he said, shoving in his third biscuit. He looked at me a little too long. And then he offered me the fourth, and I said no, although it did look like a very pretty biscuit, caramel brown on top, glistening.

All I could do in front of him was drink the tea, which was sweet like hummingbird water, and cold, and it came in a pitcher, which sat sweating on the table. There was always more of it—people would come by and fill it. There was an endless, thin supply. For a short time, the sweetness killed your hunger. That was the trick. It felt like it would last forever, while you were drinking it. Then after, instead of satisfaction, you just had an edge. I wanted the edge.

I started drawing his whole body. This took me longer. He didn't seem to mind. He held the pose twenty-five minutes, thirty, forty. I told him to get up and walk out and have a Pepsi anytime he wanted, but then I didn't take breaks—I forgot—and he didn't ask me to.

One night, very late, a few days after that lunch place, I went over to him. Close up, I saw the dampness on his brow. I ignored it. I had learned from Appleton that you ignored a model's discomforts. I reached over and turned Tim's chin a little, for there was a cleft in it, a subtle one, which I wanted in the picture. And then he kissed me.

It was not the kind I was used to, a mixer or a sock-hop kiss, from a mamma's boy, the kind who went to the University of Virginia, and came over to the girls' school, where it was easy to find a girl. He kissed me all the way into my mouth. I said, "What is it?"

"You grabbed me," he said.

I had, but just to get his chin a certain way. By then my hands were going down his sides, and he was standing. And mixed in with the turpentine in the studio was a smell, something like trees. I told him he had the wrong idea, and pulled away. "Why are you cold?" he said.

I told him I was not. I was not. No way. Just—

But then I saw the time, and I knew I'd have to ask him to walk me home. It was way past curfew, and if I couldn't get the guard to let me in—for by that time, Babette had gone to bed—I could be left out all night. So I needed Tim, as an escort.

I hated the way the world cooperated to make girls dependent, to make them need boys to walk them places. It seemed the first step in the whole conspiracy that a girl needed a man to somehow make her whole. I hated that.

In any event we were late, but the guard let me in. He wrote me up, but then he said I had to be late three times before the dean of women heard about it. I resolved never to let it happen again. This was so absurd. I was over twenty-one. The sexual revolution was finished everywhere but this university where women were still referred to as "coeds." They didn't see that. These were the house rules.

There were several chaste nights after that. I drew his limbs, his hands. I drank Pepsis. I never ate. I just couldn't make myself anymore.

The third week of classes, Appleton pulled everybody else over to show them what I was doing. I heard one say, "How did you manage to change?"

It was Peter. I wanted to go off somewhere with him and have coffee and talk and talk, for I was coming up with theories all the time, about the new figurative painters in New York. The superrealists. Then I saw a look pass over his face, like fright. That night I made Tim promise to take his breaks. I thought if I didn't treat him right, he'd get fed up. I had started planning the triptych. It was a big project. Large oil paintings of him in a variety of poses.

At one point, when we'd been going almost forty minutes, his knee fell out a little. It wasn't in the frame. I went over and grabbed his lower thigh to move it. I noticed that smell again. Like trees, but also sweet.

When I saw the time, I couldn't even pause to wash out my brushes.

He insisted on walking me home. He said he had a shortcut, through the arboretum. "You haven't seen it? Someone came up with a word for every single tree. They all have labels, even the seedlings."

You couldn't read the labels at night.

It was two in the morning when we stood up, and I wanted something to drink—sugar water. We staggered down the sidewalk on the street that bordered the campus. We had stopped short. I had a diaphragm, but not with me. Girls in girls' schools then did things like that, on spec, to be sophisticated.

I saw Appleton coming out of a bar with Peter and another girl from the class. He was drunk, and he called out, "Claire, what have you been doing?"

I saw in the plate glass of an all-night coffee shop what he meant. My hair was wet, my lips were swollen, my eyes red. I was skinny too, losing weight.

"I don't know," I said. I was laughing. But secretly, I thought I knew. I was seducing my model, the way artists did. The way Appleton did.

Tim and I went into the coffee shop and sat down. It was too late to worry about curfew, about Babette, the guard. The waitress came over and asked the two of us, with an odd tone, "What do you want?" and we both started to laugh, because the question seemed philosophical. When she was gone—for he hadn't answered—I looked at Tim and asked him what he did want. And he said, "You."

I told him I didn't love him. I didn't even know him that well, or agree with him about anything, and I had gone to a college way up in Virginia and he lived down here. I was never going home to Fayton, and we didn't really have anything in common. And I was hoping to go to art school at Yale. He asked me where Yale exactly was. "See?" I said.

"You are so far from me," he said.

I said, "Yes, that's what I'm telling you."

And he said, "No, I mean over there. Sit beside me."

"You don't want somebody like me," I told him.

"Why not?" he asked.

I tried to explain I wasn't his type. I had big plans, I had things to do.

I stayed across the table from him, watched him eat two pieces of pie. I couldn't believe how much he ate.

One night, not long after, though, we were in the arboretum. The painting had gone well. Tim was kissing me everywhere like he always did, over and over, and patient, and I felt him finally that time, reached for him, and then he was on me, as if that touch were yes. I did not say no. I had to find out, I told myself. Some secret, I told myself.

Staggering home that time, I had to lean on him. I hated that. I felt I would never be able to stand again, to have any balance at all. For how could you, really, if you were open like that, really, space inside you? Obliterated the way I felt? I felt obliterated. I was almost angry. I had always thought of myself as a solid girl, as all of one piece. With other men, I had remained that way, all of one piece, even though I'd been in their beds, done it. But not with Tim. As I might have said at the time, I had always kept "on top of it." But not with him. I climbed into my dorm through an open basement window that time. I'd run out of excuses.

I lay on my back in my plain room, staring at the ceiling, completely confused. I'd always, before, stayed aloof, in some sense. It was just like everything else: I'd been such a good girl, such a good, ambitious student. Single-minded. Focused. But in three weeks I'd lost the knack. And now, now. In the morning I went to breakfast and had coffee, cigarettes, Pepsi. Which helped, which calmed me some. I know I looked with great longing at the eggs, the donuts in the cafeteria, but I refused them. By the time I got to class I dismissed my confusion, my lapses. I was back to telling myself that certainly this wasn't knowledge, just information. You were curious about him. He was different. He touched you differently. You found out. You really are solid, solid as they come. He just knocked you off balance. It was temporary. But I went back for more.

July, after that, was a blur: no food, just painting, and depending on that open basement window. After the night in the arboretum, he still came to my studio, but he didn't really need to sit for me anymore. I had memorized his body. And I memorized the cold surface of the floor of my studio, and the printed sheets in his room at the widow's, and the way the grass in the arboretum was colorless and dark at night, how he smelled like trees.

It was mutual, I told myself when I came up for air. We were tough, we needed something from each other. I was getting over the first shock of him. It was just a trade, part of getting those paintings done. They were beautiful paintings to me then. Tim in his jeans and his Vietnam vet haircut, his long arms, his crossed knees, light from a lamp glowering down into him, as if there were something terribly interesting inside him. As if, I thought. Appleton said he looked wild, and dangerous, "unmediated." In fact, after he described my paintings of Tim in this way, Appleton told me that I had "it." He meant talent, drive, what it takes. I burst with pride, hearing that. Everything was worthwhile, if I could get Appleton to say that.

It sounds so antique to me now, the very idea, of "it."

I kept making resolutions. I would tell Tim I didn't like him like that, it was all a lot of fun, but it couldn't mean that much. We weren't a bit alike. I even asked him why he didn't get some sweet girl like himself and he said he already had one. I said I found it irritating, the way he thought of me as someone you said sweet nothings to. "You say them to me," he said. It was true, I did.

Finally, we had a huge fight, a few days into August. We broke it off. I told myself I felt relieved. It was too confusing. He had too much, what was it—influence over me. I couldn't stand it. I called him banal.

My triptych was on the first wall as you went in to the student show at the end of the summer. I'd won first place. In the painting in the center, the one I finished just as we finally decided not to see each other, his legs were out before him, and his thumb was in the belt loop of his straight-legged jeans. He was staring at the viewer, and in his eyes I had created a rebel look. At the beginning of the evening, I swaggered around the gallery in a black outfit like the one Appleton had taken up wearing. I was listening to the comments, the praise.

Then Tim came in, uninvited. The effect he had was terrible. Suddenly my paintings felt depthless to me. He mocked me— there he was, my model, walking around in 3-D. In fact, the whole goal I had come that summer to achieve, which I had achieved— Appleton thought I was marvelous, had told another professor, "she paints like a man"—were emptied, by Tim's presence in the room. I couldn't account for it.

Appleton looked at him. I wanted Tim out of there. But this was the worst—Tim drank the awful wine they were serving and stood around, and threw back his head and let them all come up to him, and tell them what he was, or what he seemed like. Based on something false. Based on my version. I wanted to protect him somehow. Peter was following him from room to room, asking questions, treating him like a specimen. Tim didn't look at me. Then, in the middle of a conversation with Appleton, he just stomped out.

I followed him home, down those same streets we'd staggered along in July, holding each other up. At the widow's, he turned on the porch and said, "What do you want now?"

"I don't know," I said.

"Go on, Claire. Go on and act it all out, Claire. What other crappy thing do you have to tell me?"

"I don't know—" I stood there in the street, crying, furious at myself for it.

When I found out, I was even angrier. Not at Tim, because I had told him I was using the diaphragm right—he'd made a point of asking. I had been careless, but what upset me most were the impudent facts. Their persistence: the facts I knew at the outset. Totally unfair.

Right before the end of the summer, I went to the gallery, where they were taking down the show. I'd just heard. Appleton was there, admiring my pictures as they were coming down, and he said, "You show his hardness, but everybody can see it's an armor—the point is what's underneath. Really, I don't know how you got that effect. Uncanny. We see one story but we know there is another one behind it."

"I'm pregnant," I said out loud for the first time.

I would always remember that gallery, which was once a bank. It was grandiose as a tomb. Appleton stayed where he was, but his features backed away. He had a long balding head, and tight olive skin. As soon as I said the words, his eyes, which were smallish and close together, spread apart and sank. His narrow nose closed up a little; his lips tightened. He seemed to be reshuffling things in his mind, putting them inside boxes, or turning shapes inside out, or right side in. His first words to me were, "How bizarre."

He did not recover from that remark—and I wanted him to, I really did. He did go on for ten or fifteen minutes. He just could not imagine that a painter as good as me, as ambitious, could do this. Become pregnant.

It was unbearable, seeing how he saw me, and so quickly—a character in one of his anecdotes—an energetic talented girl he taught once, who got knocked up by her model. *What a pity, too bad. I thought she had it.*

I felt myself collapse right before his eyes. For I was how he saw me, I still believed that. I was amazed, somehow, to be alive, after this encounter. To walk out still flesh and bone.

. . .

When forever was finally over, a nurse walked in and asked me how I had come to find myself in such a predicament. I didn't tell her the long version: Appleton, the paintings, Tim, the arboretum. I said, instead, that I had thought this couldn't happen to me. The nurse paused before the pat speech and said I seemed intelligent, and should look out for myself.

I said, "Why do you say that?"

Nothing is quite what you imagine. When I was on the table, a man was chattering at me, and a nurse was holding my hand. It took less time than they said. You don't feel there, anyway, they told me.

Several months later, I dreamt that I met Appleton on a sidewalk. He insisted he had a coin in his hand, but after I followed him for blocks, and pried apart his fingers, his palms were empty. Where? I woke up, demanding of him. Where?

When I was leaving that day, in the early afternoon, approaching Tim's truck, I started to speak, then stumbled. He took my face in his hands, and said, "What is it?"

I was going to say I was famished—they'd made me fast. But nothing looked the same as when we had gone in—the sky had cracked along the horizon, bright bands of sun seeping through. The effect was a beautiful, polarized light. Things looked too timid, and too temporary, and too vivid at once. I couldn't recall the name for this just then, but I did remember how to use it in landscape.

A certain heat brought me back to Tim's face, and in it, I saw all sorrow. With some desperation, I started to tell myself how I would render such an expression, for it was out of scale, his remorse—intense, magnetic. "It's nothing," I answered, but as I said it, I saw that sentence, that line, form a seam that was trying to hold back so much it just burst.

Pipe Smoke

Sidney Byrd, 1986

I have met up with Lily at Pauline's grave, out in the country. Lily has invited me over, so I go, happy to see her after all these years. I think she means me no harm.

She takes out her mother's best china, makes hot tea with lemon, and her parents, whom she is visiting, are at the drugstore, where they always are. She lets it steep, pours my cup. At the sight of that, her serving me, I think, well, the time has finally come when Lily and I can talk as if there had been one life in that town in those days, and not two, the one at the front door and the one at the back. But soon I learn.

We do talk about Pauline for a while, how good she was. She was my best friend in the world.

Then, second cup, Lily has a story to tell.

One day recently, since she has been living in big Washington, which she calls "DeeCee," she was driving in a small town in Virginia. This is for her job. She works at a newspaper. She passed by a cemetery with white crushed oyster shell paths. And all of a sudden she sees Cheryl Ann Sender that day her daddy was buried. "Remember?" she says. "Over in the cemetery on Sycamore?"

I have always hoped I would forget that day. I have gone whole years not thinking about it.

Then, Lily says, she was a little girl again, back in that den of Mr. Sender's, in his big lap, him with his mouth all over her face, his thick hands tearing off her clothes. The smell of pipe smoke came right in the car in Virginia. She ended up going off the road. She cried. For hours she couldn't drive.

Then Lily says, "Well, Sidney?"

"What?" I ask. I have never heard Lily was with him the day he died. The story was, it was a gun accident, but I know the truth, that it was a suicide. I know because I cleaned up after it. It still turns my stomach to think about that day.

"Did it happen?" Lily asks. In a voice so small I can hardly believe. As if she were eleven years old, instead of thirty-some.

"If you say so," I say.

"He called me Cheryl Ann," Lily says. "Then Pauline came in. I remember." Lily pauses. She is going into my eyes, I can't get her to stop. I have to look away. "But what happened next?"

For almost a minute we look at each other. Cheryl Ann comes into my mind. I have not thought of her in years. Her pointy shoulders, her white skin, the way her breasts made her top heavy, look like she might fall forward any minute. I wasn't there to see it when it was going on—I was working for the McKenzies part of that time—but her father messed with her from the time she was nine. I found this out from the notes he wrote, when Mrs. Olive forced me into cleaning up before the coroner came. He said he had a right to Cheryl, because she was his first. His, he owned her. All of her, her soul. That was love. This is what he wrote down.

I try to change the subject. Didn't Cheryl Ann move to Paris, France? Lily says she heard the same—Cheryl went over as an au pair. "Like a maid," she says.

I wonder why that girl would want to look after some other woman's children. The new movie at the Paramount was made in Paris, I say I have heard. Has Lily been to the Paramount lately? I ask.

But Lily says, "What did Cheryl's mother know? Mrs. Olive?"

I say white women back then always lied, it was 'bout all they did. And it was a long time ago, before people said everything. It is the 1980s now. Everybody talks now. She probably lied to herself, or pretended.

Lily's eyes lower a little at that. Like she don't like my answer. Well, she wants the truth, she better be ready for it, I think.

I remember Pauline just quit taking care of Lily after Mr. Sender died. That very next week. She never explained to me. Now it occurs to me it was because he bothered Lily. Maybe her parents knew, and let Pauline go, blamed her. Pauline wouldn't have fought back. She didn't have it in her. Not Pauline. Pauline suffered for that child. I think Pauline was weak.

I take a look at this Lily. She has a trim little body as a grown woman. She says she got divorced—she has no children. I asked her why. She said she and her husband just had different ideas of what a marriage was. He didn't want her to "do" anything, she says. She says she has to find herself before she can get married again. How odd that sounds to me, how trivial if you must know. Your husband is like your mother and father and you are like father and mother to him too, that's what you swear to, and you don't change your mind. That is how I was raised. That is why I haven't married, that and Raoul, my love, is dead now for a long time. Lily has a car of her own and a job. Her teeth have been straightened. She's kept her bangs, they look cute. She's gotten out of Fayton, she's had a sophisticated life. But she says, "Now I see that monster all the time."

I say, "He's dead now." I got his filthy blood off those paneled walls, off those duck decoys he collected, with the beady eyes. I still dream about it.

"My mother said nothing happened. I asked her, this week. Why would I make this up? Am I making it up?"

"That is what your mother would have to say," I say, the truth of it. But my heart is pounding. I'm mad at everybody in this story except Cheryl. Lily, I can't help but think about how she was when she was little. So hardy and eager. Convinced nothing would ever happen to her. That is how they were raised—they were lied to, so they could grow up lying to themselves. I say, "Pauline told you directly not to see him." It just comes out. Someone should defend Pauline, she let everybody push her around.

"What are you saying?" Lily says, her voice rising.

"She told you he had guns, but you were too smart for that."

"I was eleven years old. He didn't even know my name. Did he kill himself because of me?" Lily asks. "'Cause Pauline found him out, because of me?"

"Aren't you glad he's dead?" I say. I am. "This all you want to talk about?" Suddenly I don't feel like any tea. I stand up. I turn my back on Lily Stark and her imaginary pipe smoke. I march through Lily's mother's dining room, and past the silver Pauline used to spend her Fridays on, that tarnished again by Monday morning. Lily follows me, begging me to stay. She says, "But still nothing seems real. What else happened? Tell me. You know. That's the point. I don't really know. It seems as if my whole life happened to somebody else. Or didn't really happen at all. To hear my mother—"

"Look at you. What you want with it?" I say, still moving. "What you going to do with it? Play with it? Why you want me to go through all that old filth? Pauline didn't pay? She didn't have to leave this house where she worked ten, eleven years? Couldn't tell you nothing."

"That's not fair," Lily says.

"You want to talk about fair?" I ask. "Fair is a whole other subject."

At first, Lily stands in the doorway, for I have shocked her, pulled her up. I rush out and get behind the wheel, start backing out the Starks' brick drive.

But in a few minutes there's Lily in my rearview. What now.

She is running down off the porch, coming down the sidewalk, down Winter.

I'm not going more than a few miles an hour, there's a stop sign at the corner, what's the point. I wish I could speed through it.

"That's not what I want," Lily says, catching up with me, aiming her face into my rolled-down window—my AC is acting up. "That's not what I meant. I'm sorry. I'm so sorry. I am. Please, Sidney, come back. Have your tea. Please. I'm so sorry."

She's crying like a perfect child. She has not changed. "Go home, Lily Stark," I tell her. "Go talk to your mamma."

"She's dead. Pauline is dead," she says.

And that is the truth of it. It is the truth of all those girls, they had hired mammas. I hated being a hired mamma, because what happens when you are fired?

I was never like Pauline. I didn't take on their mess unless they made me. The McKenzies made me, that crazy woman, had that child Claire, and Sweetie. I was saving their lives and they didn't have the sense to keep me. I tried to stay clear after that. Then I went to the Senders.

But they always made you. They always make you. They still want to make you. As I roll forward, I believe Lily is going to keep running along the side of the car, and I dread it.

But then, I see in my rearview that she is standing there, her arms unfolded. She's stepped up in the curb, she's not going to get run down—she has that much sense. She's just watching me run away, no smile, no frown. I am running away. Wouldn't you?

I take off, get up to thirty-five. I remember Lily there weeping at Mr. Sender's burial. She was worried about everybody else: she was a little girl wanting to turn this out, get it finished, get people home. She is still the same. She should learn to mind her own life. Cheryl was stuck there by her daddy's grave. Lily made it her business. She wanted Cheryl to get in her boyfriend's car. Finally Lily got up with her mother, and went home. I was the one who had to stay by Cheryl. She was fainting, crying, I couldn't do nothing with her. She didn't ever leave with her boyfriend who had the nice car. I am not sure how she got home. It occurs to me that Cheryl Ann might still be standing there right now, in the cemetery on Sycamore, next to her daddy's stone, the Paris business is the lie. I know this can't be true, that doesn't mean it isn't.

It is natural to me to go home the old way, up Winter to Locust, over to Sycamore. It is the way I came to Lily's house. It's the way through town we always took when we were going to work for white people, for colored people had the land on the other side of that cemetery, and we still do, but it is not as sharp now, I mean the line. But I decide to go downtown instead, up Stuart Street to the bypass, swing around the whole city, past the place where I work now. It is three times longer to get to my house, but I feel like going fifty-five. I feel like seeing Fayton speed by me in a blur, looking the way something does when you erase it.

A few years after Pauline left the Starks', after old man Sender died, Mrs. Olive Sender cut me way back, saying her husband didn't leave enough life insurance. And him in that business. She had her nephew, the orphan, living with her then, as well. Tim.

She made him work. Before she went into the apartment, sent him to live with the Cobbs, I left. I was glad to leave. After that I got on at the factory where we sew baby shoes, little cloth ones. My bosses are from New Jersey and they just ask for your hands and your eyes and your eight hours. They don't ask you to be false, carry their secrets in your heart, clean up the blood, stand outside in the cold because you might be some white man's temptation. They don't want you to solve their lives and bear their meanness. They just want you to punch the clock and turn on the sewing machine, turn it off when you are done, and walk out. Think of that, they want you to walk out, forget the day.

Sometimes I think the reason white people have run from town, from us, is that we don't do that work for them anymore. They have all wandered out into the big lots, with the big houses, brick, and they are looking there for the care that we used to dose out at a dollar an hour. I don't think they've found it yet. They keep buying machines. They are still angry.

But then, some nights when I step into the parking lot, toward my Buick, look up at the stars, at the moon, see my breath, I believe it is a new world. Nothing is what it was when I was young, and I don't have anything I have to bear that belongs to them, and I am not angry, and my soul is not bitter. And some nights, like this night, after my talk with Lily, after she has wept in the street for fury, and backed away in the end, sorrowful, it is the old world that wins, and it is all stirred up. It's not my job to do it now, and I won't do it, I won't, but I have a mind to tell Lily to let them be, let them all lie down again, the devils in the earth over on Sycamore. She was calm when I last saw her. Perhaps she could hear me. I have a mind to tell Lily to take the long way round to get home if she has to, or stay away from home if it takes that. She has to find a way of seeing this all by herself. If I were to tell her, I wouldn't say

it was easy but you can try. But I'm not going to tell her. It is someone else's job.

She is not going to hear it from me that the past doesn't have to
hold you. Even though it wants to so bad, sneaking in with pipe
smoke, with oyster shells. But that is the truth, I think. I tell
myself the past will not hold me.

. . .

But then a week later I go to the movies.

There was a time when black people could only sit in the bal-
cony at the Paramount downtown. It was awful up there—rats
were living on dropped popcorn, whole families. They cleaned it
up in the seventies, after civil rights, and opened up seating to
everyone, of course. But I have a memory and wouldn't go for
years. After I saw Lily, I was feeling low, couldn't sleep, and somebody talked me into the picture, said the movie was funny, and
how else was I going to see Europe, or was I planning on joining
the army? I sat in front, in a nice red upholstered seat. After a
while, a little white actress was walking across a bridge over the
Seine River in Paris in a dress with crinolines underneath, made
of tulle like that we used to wash and starch for the girls in the
families in Fayton. Those girls looked as if everything below their
waists was clouds when we were done dressing them.

It happened when people all around me were giggling. Something was funny, but suddenly I stopped following. For no reason
having to do with the plot, I got the idea the actress was going to
fall into the water. The other people on the screen didn't know it,
but they were all going into the river too. And the people in the
audience, the laughing people, black and white, were about to go
in as well. I could feel them all tumbling forward, going down, and
wasn't anybody, once they fell in, ever, ever going to touch the bottom. There was no bottom, that was the thing.

I knew I was going to say something, call out, scream in the theatre. My heart was pounding. I had to get up and run. I didn't even take my Raisinets—I didn't stop till I was on the street. Main Street, Fayton, eight-thirty at night, was not alive, not like it used to be. Hardly a soul, only thing rolling was a police car. It was the Technicolor, I finally decided, after I'd walked a few blocks, looked into a few store windows. That river was too blue. It was blue like the heart of blue, and cold. I couldn't bear to look at it. But it drew me. I couldn't bear to look away.

. . .

Once, when Pauline was confined to bed, first time the doctor said she had a congestive heart condition, I went to see her. This was many years after Pauline had left the Starks', and she had almost finished raising Tamara, that baby of her sister's she hauled down from Philadelphia, ended up sending to Duke college. Pauline was in her back room, in a white cotton smock, lying on a low couch, in the dark in the middle of the day. Those last years, she usually wore a big Afro wig, but it was on top of a lamp on a small table that day. She had her hair wrapped in a white rag. She didn't like people to see her like that but she always let me come in. We got to talking about all the marching, about the riots. Things were going on then, Dr. King was dead, the schools were opened up, and white people were mad about it. I whispered, "We really don't have to take on the mess they hand us now. We get to let that go. They going to have to take back all that meanness." I breathed better just saying it. "That's why they really so mad."

"Oh," Pauline said, then she made a strange sound, almost like a laugh, a laugh of relief, of an unexpected gift. I wondered whether she had heard me. If she knew what I'd meant. She seemed half asleep, and I had been going on. Or was it a little cry. As if she felt how much *they* must carry, now, how hard it is *for them.* That was Pauline, putting herself in the shoes of other people. But I wasn't sure.

That night I had a dream. I saw a huge weight on Pauline, like all that fluid on her chest, I thought at first. I felt I could pry it off. It would kill her if it stayed there. I could save her. So I went up to her, and I pried it away, but then I saw the place it left, exposed, and bloody: a fresh and terrible wound. Then that closed over, with something that grew into a skin, but then it was happening again, the weight was coming back. I pried off that new skin, and saw another wound, and then another growth came, and I pried off that, and another. I was going to save her, I knew I was strong. But for a moment, I paused, exhausted—I was fearful this labor would never stop. I would have to get back to it, though, for Pauline was certainly going to die, this would kill her. Then I started to feel something so hard to feel I told myself to look away. But I looked back at my friend. She was breathing, Pauline was breathing. She was alive, wide alive.

The wound had become an enormous eye—big as a baby, and as open to the world.

Salvage

Homer Cobb, 1999

We set out about midnight, which is late, I know, but Aunt Isabel didn't think we had much time to find him.

To get to North Salter you head south from Fayton through the Alba River Basin on 117 toward Guston Corners to State Road 20A. This is by far the loneliest beach road I know of. Long time ago the island was a place for pirates to hide their booty and now mamma sea turtles come to shore there to bury their eggs. Later, on a schedule, the turtles come out of the sea to greet their babies just as they hatch, eager to show them all their love and how to live in the ocean. People time their vacations to see this happen, but I have never been there for it.

The papers she'd downloaded were on her lap. She kept turning on the lamp in my truck to read the names of the cottages to me. "Dune's End ring a bell? Ocean Destiny Townhomes? Turtle-watch?" She announced which beach rentals she'd try first. It was early May, not the high season, and he would have had his choice of properties. She'd isolated the oceanfront condos because her son, Bit, had always liked to stare at the waves when he was a boy.

He was fifty that March, but she assumed he still had the same tastes.

As we were getting toward Blalock where they grow blueberries she started telling me about him: that he was a footling breech, for example. She was only eighteen when she had him and this was before the time of drop-of-the-hat cesareans. There was probably a way to get him out quicker, but what did she know, she was a child in labor. She hadn't wanted to marry his father, my uncle Tulip, really. She had always done the best she could: did I know how hard it was being a mamma when you see your own child is inclined to bring suffering to himself and those who love him? And I said yes, ma'am, it must be hard. I had said this before.

She was difficult for me to contradict. I was her favorite nephew. She was sixty-eight years old, and used to getting her way. And not just from her husband: people whisper in Fayton, about her going to Sorrowsville and Pine Sands in her thirties, and forties, and even fifties, and being seen coming out of motels, or standing round truck stop restaurants with her raven hair up, sunglasses on, her sweaters lowcut. She is old now, but she can still throw herself at strangers.

At the one stoplight in Moscow there is a worn-down gas station and next to it a café I know where old men sit around from six until two on weekdays, and eat plate lunches with sides of collards—still, in the year 1999. When we passed it—at 12:40 a.m., so of course it was closed—Aunt Isabel said, "Let's stop for coffee, we have a long night ahead of us." I said okay though I knew there wasn't much on that road.

Back in January when he still seemed well, her son, my cousin Bit, and I visited in a gourmet pizza restaurant in Dimeboro, near Oleander where the university is. It was in a part of that town they have really New Yorked up, which didn't bother him. He hadn't come back to Carolina because he cared about it, out of homesickness for the old places. Nostalgia is my profession: I go out before they tear down a house for a Popeye's or a Savamart and take away the old doors and the shutters and the stained glass and the newel posts. I strip and sand them until they are beautiful again, and sell them. I call this Homeboy's Salvage. Everybody calls me Homeboy. Aunt Isabel is the reason.

He wanted to reminisce, which could have been a sign. He told me about the time in the last of the sixties when he lived as a squatter in a condemned house on a canal in Holland. He got the Amsterdam government to agree he was an artist, pay him money he mostly spent on hashish and heroin. His friends did videos of naked people standing in the North Sea yelling in Dutch about everything that was wrong with their lives, he said. The films were about the point of life, which is to become transparent, he said — he wrote the electronic music — and I had no idea what he was talking about.

As I was leaving, I had a feeling he was falling in somehow. I felt the impulse to catch him. But then what would he think, I thought. We were just shooting the shit. I made a point of visiting him every year around the holidays since he'd taken that job at State, sort of a glorified sound man, and an instructor. I was the only blood relative besides his sister who was talking to him. As I left him I did mention he should see a doctor, he seemed too thin, but he said he had, and had been told it was anxiety. He was supposed to take his Prozac but being on that stuff was like living in a rubber.

I pulled in at a Timesaver ten miles out from Moscow, still an hour-plus from the island. Aunt Isabel stayed in the car while I went in and brought out two coffees. She said hers wasn't hot, was there anything I could do? I told her I didn't think so, and was relieved when she changed the subject. She asked me if I was sure they took that orange van. I said they must have, but I didn't say I had seen them drive away. "Well, that will be easy to spot," she said, summing up and taking charge the way she likes to. When we started rolling she turned down her window and poured out half her cup, and this pissed me off some, but I let it go.

I was real little when he was in Europe, and then later, when I was about five, he was in California with a rock band—always the black sheep. When I was eleven, my parents told me he was in New Mexico in recovery from the bad things he took, and we were visiting him, driving across the country. Around Amarillo going west on I-40 the land turns red-brown and the rocks poke up out of it like parts of bodies, elbows, shoulders, heads, like a giant has been exploded, and there are the fragments that have survived. I thought someone ought to put these huge parts back together, thought you could do it if you had a big enough crane, strong enough trucks, enough will power. I had it all worked out: one was a shoulder, one a knee, another a big old head. I was still on this project as we pulled up at the hospital.

My parents went into the main office to get visitors' passes. I couldn't wait. I unlocked the car and ran out into the garden among men sitting in iron chairs staring at a three-humped mountain. I had to find out if I would know him—I'd never laid eyes on him before.

Near the fork in the road near Snyder's Ferry, Isabel said, "The parking is underneath the cottages in these places. So we'll have to get out and search each driveway." She meant to find the van he'd come in. It wasn't going to be easy. "Thank god they don't allow high-rises," she said, for once you spotted the car in a big parking lot how would you ever figure which unit he was in? "Knock on every door at this hour? Now that would be *hard*."

As if what we were planning to do were easy: ride up and down an island at three in the morning, searching for a single man and his allies in some unknown rented house. A man who was fast asleep at least, who had no intention of being found.

That day in February after I got the call about Bit's surgery, I drove up there quick as I could, but then I got lost in the hospital. It seems to me still they make every medical complex like that into a maze on purpose. You have to thread your way through useless elevators and bridges and wrong wings before you get to the right place, where they tell you the answer, Life or Death. By the time I found the oncology floor Bit was in post-op and his surgeon was coming down the hall—a short man, who worked out, you could tell. He started off telling me about the tumor in Bit's gut and on his liver and how they got it all. "He's just a young man, he's a young man," he said, and I said Cousin Bit was about to have a big birthday.

That's when the little surgeon started to weep.

When I finally got in the room, a woman told me Bit would be glad to see me when they brought him in. He'd be in his room in half an hour, she said. She was a big person, wearing rose-colored stone earrings you might see on Home Shopping Network. She had a smocked shirt and stretch pants, tight and fuschia. But I didn't see her as fat or ugly, which I suppose she is and was. Something told me I was in the presence of a blazing person. This was true, really, till the end: Harriet had a pink fire, and guarded Bit, but I am getting ahead of myself. I asked her how she knew my cousin. She worked with him; she was the tech secretary.

A little later, the oncologist came in, Dr. Layton, a tall woman, bony and smart. Harriet asked, "How long?"

"Months," she said quietly.

I said to her, "What gives you the right to say that? What?" Harriet looked at me to let me know I was yelling. I could tell what she was thinking, right off. I communicated with her well the whole time, up to a certain point.

There is a long stretch from Alba Hill to Wallville with not much to see, in fact, the soil is sand and like a barrens, and spooky. To grow anything in the land you have to supply all the nourishment, the earth is spent. People put it into soybeans or tobacco. If you turn due south in Wallville you pass through Mitchellboro, which has a lake in it formed by a meteor. In fact that whole part of the state was bombarded with parts of an exploded planet eons ago and if you think about it, it does a pretty good job of covering this up, of looking normal, although all the lakes are suspiciously perfect ovals. During this period in the trip Aunt Isabel started to sleep in spite of our coffee. I noticed how pretty her features are, how fine and how like her handsome son's, in spite of all her face-lifts.

When I told her about Bit's surgery in January the first thing she wanted to know was if he had a bag like Loretta Young. I didn't know who that was. Found out later they didn't bother to change his plumbing. I drove her up to the hospital the first time. She hadn't seen Bit in more than ten years, it was that bad. But there at first, he seemed calmed, even gratified, by her presence. Dr. Layton came in to say they weren't going to give him radiation. He was getting little pills instead. When Bit asked for some time with the doctor alone, we stepped outside.

Harriet said, "Don't you realize what they did? They went in there and took what they could. Just sewed him back up. They like to say they got it all. Bull. Don't you think they would have taken his whole gut if they thought he had any time?" And she started to break up.

Isabel looked at her the way she can look, and she said, "Excuse me, are you a doctor?"

For about ten days there Bit was recovering at State Memorial, and then in his little apartment outside Oleander, in a complex where a lot of Mexicans lived. We couldn't get him to talk or eat. When I would go over I'd see his sister, Dora, telling him how green magma and shark cartilage or the extract of the interior of apricot pits would surely save his life. If not that a faith healer who was coming to Rockborough to the True Vine Church would save him. She had a series of testimonies to that fact in her enormous purse, which she read to him. On the eleventh day he told her he would rather not go to Rockborough. He would like to get a bunch of movies he really loved, and watch them over and over.

Then Uncle Tulip came up. He didn't even visit until he had found what he thought was the solution. He announced he had discovered the best doctor in the world for Bit's kind of cancer. This man was in Houston, and money was no object. When he said that it gave me shivers, for money has always been the object to Uncle Tulip. He took Bit down there with his mother in a jet a friend of his owned. Bit was willing: he wanted to live, to believe.

The doctor made them wait four days for all the test results. And they tolerated each other well, I heard, father and son, mother and son. Even mother and father, which was quite a feat. For my aunt and uncle fight like dogs—I've seen it my whole life, and they are famous all over Fayton for it. The three went out together, played video poker, sat in restaurants, looked at CNN. Same parents hadn't spoken to him in a decade before that spring, imagine.

Finally they called them in and said the doctors at State Memorial were absolutely right. The disease was too advanced, basically.

"What I pay you good money for?" Uncle Tulip said, lunging for the doctor. That's when my cousin Benedict got up and left. He punched the elevator buttons and went down before they could catch him. He set out walking on the avenue in his hospital gown.

After a few blocks he collapsed. They had to admit him for dehy-
dration. They put him on Xanax, which Harriet never liked.

In February after Aunt Isabel had that confrontation with
Harriet she went home to Fayton and told everybody her son had
rampant colon cancer. In town people said how sorry they were. In
March Isabel stood up in the Methodist church to ask the congre-
gation to pray. For this occasion, I noticed she had a white lock in
her hair, a little gray slice like a skunk stripe. This was brand new:
all my life Aunt Isabel had dyed her hair pure black. My wife,
Paula, said the streak was to make her look stricken, to attract
attention. I said Isabel was trying. Paula said yes she was, but look
what she has to work with.

I told Paula that wasn't fair.

Soon after, Isabel suggested that Bit move out of his apartment
complex. The reason was, Isabel was uncomfortable there. He had
been docile and subdued since he returned to Houston, and he
agreed. She found a good-looking furnished condo near the hospital. She spent over one thousand dollars in Linens 'N Things to
domesticate this place, with four-hundred-thread-count sheets and
so forth. I know because I took her. She declared she would never
leave his side, but she averaged about two days a week in Oleander.
When she was there, she encouraged him, made him take his
pills. She told him he looked well, which was a lie. She hired a
practical nurse who came in the mornings. I was proud of Isabel,
proud of the family, how it came around, which I took to be the silver lining in this. Dora visited often, loaded down with tons of
advice. But usually, after about an hour, she would start to cry.
Sometimes we all wished she would take her shark cartilage and
go. In the end she left on a yoga retreat. Isabel was tougher, and I
admired that.

Down closer to the coast the pine forests open out into the lowland swamps. There are no buildings, and late at night, the horizon is only an idea, and the only lights are the cars, except at two-something in the morning there are no cars. On this stretch, Aunt Isabel woke at one point, to say to me, "Why did he leave? Really? Do you have the answer?"

I generally went up to visit Bit after Isabel had gone home for the week. Her presence put a damper on any fun we might have. She dominated the TV: House and Garden, Lifetime. Thursday night, or Friday, Harriet or her musician sons, Terry and Lucas, brought videos. We watched movies I didn't even know existed—weird, like *Persona*, and *Wings of Desire*. People in these movies talked right out of the screen at you. They got obsessed with things other people say don't make any difference—dreams, notions. Bit said that was why he liked them. Part of me could see it.

At a certain point Tim Carter got in touch—the orphan Bit had always said before that Uncle Tulip had brought in to shame him, replace him. I let the man in, but I thought they might get into a fight. For a while Bit was stiff in his chair, and tense, and Tim was the same, hunched over at the tippy end of the bum recliner we had. But then I went in the kitchen for some beer, and I heard this loud shout. I rushed in and Bit was whirling a tiny blue swimsuit about that Tim had brought in a bag—apparently it belonged to Bit when he was a boy, Aunt Isabel had bought it. Tim was returning it. Bit hurled it out a window. Tim was laughing 'til he almost fell back in that chair—it wasn't locked, and we'd seen it tip. I was surprised when Bit grabbed him, to keep him from going down, for Bit was weak. Tim took it well. Tim Carter was working in Charleston then, giving rich people fairy tale kitchens. He's a great cabinetmaker. He was seeing Claire McKenzie, after what he called a "thirty-year hiatus"—she was the visiting artist at the university museum that year, one of Fayton's claims to fame, so we saw her too—she was quiet, shy, not what you'd expect. Not haughty, the opposite, I'd say. Bit liked her. I liked her. Something about her held you like a magnet.

Tim talked to Harriet's sons a lot those same weeks, about being in a rock band, which he had done on two continents. It was all the attitude, he said, and the music, and not the money, or even the women. Harriet told them to listen.

After the swamp opens out, you see more inlets and bays on either side. Then you take a long low arch over the Intercoastal Waterway. At a blinking light you go due east on 221. Then you are in North Salter, only incorporated as a town in the last ten years. Until recently, people didn't think of it as much of a beach. The only cottages there were isolated at the southern point, where the sound reaches around. The water is rough at North Salter, and there are rocks, which are very rare for the Carolinas. As time goes on, though, people don't notice things they used to, and will settle anywhere. Also, the whole place is being washed away, the beach eroding like crazy, and oceanfront places that used to have a wide strand in front are now standing out in the water at high tide. A few have sunk into the sea. Some say the island won't even be there in fifty years, and in fact they can prove it, but people who build on beaches nowadays do not consider the future any more than they do the past.

Other people started coming by, people who knew Bit from long ago before. They'd come on the nights we looked at the movies, it was sort of open house. I have had my resentful feelings about Bit's old friends on occasion—all the ones who left Fayton in the sixties, bewildered their parents, tried to be something important, or just wild, or both. But I let that go for a while.

A woman I had never seen drove up from Savannah where she teaches French in a college. She was prim and had long hair even though she was over fifty. She felt like a girl to be around—didn't wear any makeup. After a while you could tell she might have been beautiful but had never wanted people to know it. We watched a movie about a little boy in Europe, then she told me she knew Bit in Paris and he saved her life. She didn't say how. When she left, he told me, "Once, in 1979, on the Île de la Cité, she ordered red wine. I wasn't even snorting then. Smack is supposed to be love, but love is better." That was all he said, so I asked, and he said, "The Older Woman. Cheryl Sender. For about ninety minutes, everything was absolutely perfect."

And I knew exactly what he meant. I had no idea how.

It was about midnight when we turned away from the main crossroads in North Salter, with the town hall and the fire station and the sunglasses and boogie board emporiums. We left the main drag and dropped down onto Inlet Drive, which led to the first place on Isabel's list. A cottage, all by itself, next to a bare lot of low scraggly dunes, with heavy shrubs in front. "That's Dune's End. Park, park," she said, for she saw there was a car underneath, and light above, in the kitchen. "What 'cha think, Homeboy?"

No matter how old you get, it is always a marvel, the first time you get out of your car at the ocean. The sound, you don't want to talk over it, you want to wait a minute. But I rushed over to peek around the bushes. The car was a Mitsubishi SUV, not Harriet's sons' van, and my aunt's face fell when I told her.

"If I were him I would have picked that place," she said. "It has every amenity, and the price is right."

When she came up to Fayton to stay with Bit at the condo she always wanted to get something to make things nicer. Nothing was good enough as it was. She couldn't stand Harriet, either. She got upset with Bit, especially when he mentioned what was really going on. She called it depressing. She only talked to him about getting better. She reminded him to take his little pills from Dr. Layton which wouldn't kill a wart on a big toe, Harriet told me, much less rampaging colon cancer. Harriet's sister, a nurse in Myrtle Beach, had told her what we all had to look forward to—it broke my heart. When I tried to tell Aunt Isabel she would have none of it. She dragged him to the hospital any time he refused to eat, or felt pain, which was often. She told the doctors they better do something for him. She told Bit whatever new pills they gave him to shut her up were going to make him better, and he should improve his attitude. She insisted upon him being admitted two times for more tests that the doctors didn't even want to order. Both times when the results came back—invariably more bad news—she left him in the hospital room, and tore around Oleander and Dimeboro in her BMW for hours, until she could face it all again.

Then she'd call me up when she came home and say, "He doesn't want to live, Homeboy—he's giving up, why? Doesn't he want to fight? He weighs one hundred and two pounds now, you know what he started at?"

I said I didn't know what he used to weigh. I didn't think it was his fault.

"One sixty one," she said, exasperated. "Think of that."

Over the course of late March and through April, a great deal of stuff collected in the closets in the condo. There were clothes she'd bought him, which he had never put on. Mostly when we saw him he wore flowing pajamas that didn't disturb his terrible scar. There were slippers galore and small appliances in boxes, like a humidifier, and a blender, and a food processor, and a machine to take away the negative ions or something. There were several feng shui fountains and aromatherapy candles and tiny Zen gardens, too, but nobody had ever bothered to take these out of their boxes.

In the kitchen there were many bags of microwave popcorn for the movie nights. We stopped holding them in late April because it got hard for him to sit up through an entire feature. There were cans of soup and meal replacements and vitamins and flat crackers for the days he was nauseated and all kinds of cancer-fighting tea, and calming-down tea. It seemed as if every time I went up there, the closets were fuller, and Bit was skinnier.

We rolled past the Gulls Perch Townhomes, which seemed a little seedy, and I felt happy to find Bit hadn't settled there. But Isabel sighed, for they were the cheapest on the list and she said, "I figured Harriet would have picked them." Then she said, her spirits rising, "Let's try Ocean Destiny," a little before I was ready to hear it. In the dome light I read my watch: time, 3:25, date, 05-02. At the next corner, I hesitated, for the green sign outside did not read "Ocean Destiny Lane."

"Well, it has to be. It just has to be," she insisted.

The night had gotten very long. I said to her, "Why you think everything is just like it is on your map?"

The Monday before our wee-hour search, in the end of April, Bit stopped eating entirely. Aunt Isabel insisted he go into the hospital so he could be fed intravenously. She said he needed his strength to fight this thing. He was due to be admitted Tuesday morning. I went up to get him ready. When I rang the bell, Harriet came to the door, her arms full of blankets. Inside, there was a big sheet spread out like a picnic blanket in the living room, with two open duffle bags on it. There were plates stacked up and little piles of underwear and slippers, and about fifteen boxed videos, as well as an IV pole, two cases of Ensure, and all his pills and teas.

"Even the Xanax has him throwing up. He's off it. He called me last night and told me what he wanted to do," Harriet said before I could speak.

"You can't leave," I said.

"Why not?" she said. She was flaming red, brilliant. I couldn't bear this, so I took her face in my hands. Finally, with the touch, the solidity of it, I saw an ugly woman, tight about the face, two chins, unhappy, no husband anymore, in love with Bit in some way, I told myself, desperate for drama in her life. I thought all these things about her, and I tried hard to hate her. I suppose, in that moment, I did.

I said, "This is insane. He's ours. He belongs—"

"Hear what you are saying, Homer," she said. "You leave now or you sit there on the couch and say nothing."

"Where are you going?"

"We aren't telling you," she said. "He doesn't want you to tell them. My sister Lorelei is coming. We have everything we need, instructions from the hospice."

"What did Dr. Layton say?"

"That no matter what we do the outcome will be the same."

I couldn't stand hearing that.

Just then the bedroom door opened and my cousin emerged, a peacock-blue jacket cast over his shoulders like a cape. Instead of a shirt he was wearing a black turtleneck of Dora's—none of his own clothes would fit him. Jutting out from the too-short sleeves were his long hands, all bone with translucent skin stretched over. What you could see of his face was his flint-pointed nose and his jaw, which jutted out. I was real conscious of his teeth. He was wearing those big sunglasses, wide, Roy Orbison style. A six-foot dragonfly.

"This is crazy," I said.

"Man, I just can't be here," he told me, as he started to bend slowly, apparently in great pain, toward the recliner before him. "Let me go. I have to clear out," he said. "You know, clear out?" Settling in the chair.

"What am I supposed to say to the family?"

Harriet's two sons bustled in just then, having come up from the van to get more loot to pack. Bit commanded the situation like a king, gesturing for them to ignore certain objects. "Less is more, Terry," he said to the taller one, the blonde boy. "Didn't I tell you that?" Terry put down what he'd just piled in his arms, and stood, a sentinel.

"Go, cousin," Bit said to me.

In that moment, I could not refuse him. I went back to my truck. From my cab I watched them load the orange van, which Harriet's sons used for their rock band, called the DREAMCYCLE, but pronounced like the popsicle. It took four more trips, for nothing was in boxes. On each trip Terry gave me a high five—he was watching me—I knew to keep my distance. Bit came down at the last, leaning on Harriet, not steady. The sun seemed to shake him. I watched as they slammed all the doors and pulled into the street that blended up a hill into another street that led to a mall and then the interstate, which could have led them to Dimeboro or Clarksboro or Fayton, or anywhere, really. I was crying too hard to follow them. After a while I consoled myself that this was some sort of game and they would soon come to their senses. I had a key to the place and I went in there: it was a wreck. The bags they had left, the stacks of dishes Bit had rejected, the clothes and cast-off medicines and magazines and shoes and slippers and hundred-dollar pajamas from his mamma—all he'd determined he wouldn't need where he was going. The closets were bursting: Isabel's were full of the caretaker outfits she'd bought, but hadn't worn: dry-cleaned blue jeans, little cotton sweaters, rows and rows and rows still in their sheaths of cellophane. The place looked like what is left after a disaster, the kind of thing I usually could work with, make something out of. I didn't have the heart.

Thursday Aunt Isabel called. She believed Bit had been readmitted to State Memorial. I hadn't told her any different. At first she thought it was a mistake of the hospital's they had no record of him. She had spent all morning asking people, then she went to the condo and figured it out. I said I didn't know anything. Tulip called me back.

I have a hard time keeping a secret from Uncle Tulip and Aunt Isabel.

The news didn't rile Tulip a whole lot. He hadn't seen that much of Bit after Houston—he kept saying he'd visit, but things always came up.

Isabel asked me, "Homeboy? What's got into you?"

I cared and I cared and I didn't care right then, which spooked me. I felt ashamed.

"What more can we do for him, Isabel?" Tulip said. "He's always been this way."

Isabel said, "You never loved him."

And Tulip rose up to her, "I loved him goddamn it when you let me," and his face turned red. "He's a grown man, if you love him, and he wants to go like this, let him go, for Christ's sakes."

And Isabel said, "He's my son. He's mine."

That was when she turned to me.

I drove home, full of my mission, and talked to my wife who thought the whole thing was a little sad, and slightly funny. I pleaded Aunt Isabel's side. I owed Aunt Isabel a lot, including my livelihood. She was the one who explained me to Tulip, the one who had given me my nickname, who had given me money every Christmas since I could remember, little checks in envelopes, addressed to her dear boy. My aunt Isabel had to see her son, take care of him, it just wasn't right for Bit to take off like that for spite, I said.

"Why you always have to drag everybody back into the house, *Homeboy?*" my wife asked me. She was talking about something that happened when I was four. A story I had always been proud to tell. "Why is it always you?" she asked me.

"What is the matter with him?" I said. "Can't he just love them? He have to stick it to them the last thing he does? Haven't they suffered enough? That whole gang, his generation, make me sick. Stick it to their suffering parents and what they stood for till the bitter end, never let them off the hook. What? This life not good enough for them? Took all those drugs to get out of it, fucked everybody they saw? Left us this mess?"

"He hasn't suffered?" Paula said to me with her sweet dark eyes. "Now they haven't been trying to buy him back when he's a dying man, doesn't want to die like their boy?"

"How you know how long he has?" I asked, but I could see I wasn't getting very far with that. So I said, "Why does everybody in this family have to act out all the time? Why can't people just quiet down and be civil? You too?"

"You are the one yelling, Homer," she said. And I went out, set off to find where Harriet had taken him. I didn't know where she lived. I drove up to the university and asked around. I got to Harriet's place at five. Her little brick house with a screen door, Nissan in the carport at the side. Tomato plants in the backyard. Sweet, to be honest. I almost wanted to go inside and drink some iced tea with her, although I remembered I was mad as fire.

I managed to break in, something I've learned how to do from my years of working with abandoned properties. There was a dog dish but no dog, and a kitchen that hadn't been changed since about 1965—knotty pine. Avocado refrigerator, a real collector's item. Clean beds, quiet living room, a doily or two, some romance novels. By the phone in the kitchen though, a clue: brochures for a few beach realtors. I used my cell to make the calls, find out which one had rented to Harriet Forester, saying I was her brother and was needing to get in touch.

Third call, I got close. Marcie at Sand and Sea of North Salter found Harriet's name on their computer.

That's when I felt the hand on my neck.

Lucas, Harriet's shorter boy, thicker, and stronger. The bass, not the vocals. "What the hell you think you doing here, man?"

"She stole my cousin," I said.

"Well, the police gonna come here and steal you right now. Come back for an amplifier, find you've broken into my kitchen?"

I opened my hands, backed toward the door. "Where are they?" I said. "I want—"

He paused a second. "This is my mamma's house. You want me to cut you? That bitch Isabel want to buy her son like she bought you? Get out," he said, raising his hand. I dropped my cell running out, didn't think I could go back for it.

The loneliness of a haphazard beach town off-season can seem physical, palpable, something you would like to avoid if possible in this life. It was about three-fifty in the morning. We'd given four more properties the drive-by. None of them seemed occupied: Dunewalk, Super Sea, Gullsperch, even a little old cottage I remembered from when I was a boy, Conched Out. Isabel and I were on the main drag, again, and I was thinking about the queen palms they are always planting on this island so they can pretend it is jolly like Florida is supposed to be when the truth is it isn't.

I was getting lost again looking for the complex called Turtle-watch I and II. She picked that moment to ask me again why her son had never loved her. Why he had taken all that dope, why he ran away after all she had given him, and I was still trying to answer those questions, although it suddenly felt very late to be trying.

This is the story Paula was talking about: my daddy, Tulip's younger brother, Honey Cobb, has always found being normal something hard. He has worked for his brother his whole life, building houses, ordering around painters and paperhangers and plumbers' helpers whose hold on the basics is just about as loose as his own. One time when I was four he was sitting on the porch holding a brown bottle. He was talking to the workmen really loud. The last time I saw him doing that, I knew he stalked off with them, and they went into a car, driving rough. My mamma screamed. Not too long after, one of the tires came off the car, so the axle broke and there were sparks in the street. The car skidded, and went into a tree. My daddy had to climb out. He was bleeding from his jaw. Red blood on my own father's shirt. So this time, I took his hand and pulled him into the living room and said, "Daddy, Mamma really really really wants you to have something to eat. Let those other men play at somebody else's house now." And then he kissed me and followed me into the house, and said, "You know how to take care, don't you, son?" And my chest bloomed like a bed of jonquils. And when Aunt Isabel heard the story from my mamma she said, "You have such a good boy, Muriel, such a homeboy." Every other time I could think of that my wife, Paula, and I had shared that story I felt it was a good one. She'd never challenged me about it.

As I drove, I was considering how these trees above were on their way down the path of all true palms in this part of the Carolinas. It gave me some kind of satisfaction in that moment: no matter what anybody did to save them, a good freeze or a low-grade hurricane would come within a few seasons. They were going to keel over no matter how many nurserymen came out to prop them up, no matter how many thousands they spent to pretend North Salter was in the tropics. It wasn't in the tropics, and it wasn't even going to be here in fifty years. That gave me satisfaction too.

A double set of low-rise condos with wide balconies and two pools appeared before us. In front, a big lit-up sign in aqua and beach gray read Turtlewatch, A Sand and Sea Development. So I parked. This was the last one on the first page of Aunt Isabel's list. It didn't look promising to me—I said I'd give it a quick walk-through.

"Let me come with you," she said. "It's creepy out here."

"No," I said. "Stay."

"Okay," she said, in that offended voice she has.

But she has a point, I thought, when I set out on that black lawn. I thought of caretakers and guards, and dogs. The fourth garbage can I crept around, I found I wasn't wrong: a security light came on, and a lone Cadillac Escalade began to whoop and wail. I had to dash for my truck. Back on the main road, certain the North Salter private patrol would be rounding any corner, I insisted we park in a secluded spot. We could get some rest, start over after sunrise.

"We have to finish what we start," Isabel said.

"You drive then," I said.

"It's manual?" she asked, looking at my clutch. It had been a long time since she'd driven stick, probably half a century.

"I am tired, I'm going to have a wreck or get busted," I said.

She said, "Don't be chicken, Homeboy. Let's go on."

"And get them after us?" I asked.

"I know he's there," she said. "I can feel it."

I wouldn't drive. She started back talking about how ungrateful her son was. He had everything as a child: a swimming pool and plaid curtains in his room to match the bedspread, and fancy military school. Took such offense when they tried to help that orphan. And she bailed him out of trouble so many times, until they just got tired of it. What did he want, she went on—I had heard this all my life—to sing in rock bands, skip out on the draft, be an addict like his father's brother. She had never understood him, never. "He wants to die, to give up. I can't understand that. I always wanted to live. Isn't that what is natural? Has he always been unnatural? He's always just been trying to die?"

"He's dying to get away from you," I said. I couldn't believe what I'd said. "I'm sorry," I said. "Sorry. I didn't mean it."

Without a second's hesitation she turned and slapped me on the face. "You can't put this on me. You bastard. As much as I have given you. As much—"

"But you are so wrong," I said. I couldn't help it. I didn't want to, in a way, but I said it, "You have everything wrong. You see everything wrong, wrong, wrong." I felt as if this part of me, inside, this other mouth, this other head, in where my heart was, was talking. I had felt it before but I almost always keep it quiet. I was just too tired to keep it quiet.

"Get out," she said.

I realized we were down at the end of the island, where the big old cottages were. The ones that were built before I was born. I didn't think any of these had made Isabel's list: most were not on the market. The few that were rentals were very expensive.

I got out in the dark. That one inside me was overjoyed, jubilant. I ran across the road and took off my shoes and darted between two big places, and then another row, and a third, until I got to the strand. Let her find him, I thought. I couldn't help her anymore. I walked along the edge of the surf. It was about four-thirty. At some point I dove into the dark ocean with my clothes on, and swam straight out into the waves. I used to swim out like this as a boy. It was dangerous, especially when there was an undertow. When I was nine, ten, eleven, I would think, no matter what I do they will still be miserable. All them up there at that cottage. For we vacationed together in the summer, either on this island or at Myrtle. My father and my uncle Tulip and my mother and Aunt Isabel and I would all go together, sometimes Bit's sister, and my older brothers. Every year Aunt Isabel would flirt on the pier with strangers and Uncle Tulip would take us to dinner and pretend like it didn't matter she called him names, said she despised him. She'd laugh and say it was a joke, that she didn't mean it. Then he'd start picking on my daddy, and even my mother. They would all fight, put each other down. But we were dependent upon them in so many ways, so we had to sit there and take it, and it went on like that, on and on and on. And no matter how it hurt me, no matter what I tried to say or do, they would go on. With that cruelty.

I got out of the water. I wasn't sure where I was. I hadn't thought, consciously, come on, you need to get out, you are cold, you are drowning: what are you thinking, swimming in your clothes before dawn. None of that seemed to be part of my conscious life. There was little really left of my conscious life. I came out pretty much where I'd gone in, maybe a few hundred feet down. I looked up at the old cottages I'd run past. It was clear the sea was taking them back now with a vengeance. There were no dunes before them. There had been many when I was a boy. I noticed one double A-frame with the surf right beneath its pilings, rushing up right under the house.

That's when I saw it, the silhouette of the DREAMCYCLE VW van—so antique it could not be mistaken. There was another truck as well, on the patch of asphalt left under that unprotected cottage.

I saw her standing under the one street lamp, which had just gone out. She'd figured it out, too. She was staring up at the rickety stairs, standing next to a copse of sea oats. She was trying to stiffen her face, tie her hair back with a kerchief in the beach wind. But—

She wasn't Isabel as I knew her. She was tiny to me, frightened, terrified, frozen by her life. Petrified by what the world might think of her, what I might think of her. Cringing in fear of the very air, and not all the way human, but heartbroken. I saw her from that face inside me, that face that could see now. I went over to her.

"Ho!" came from up at the top of the steps. I turned and saw Terry in his sleeveless shirt, his flip-flops. Except he looked more glinty and majestic than Terry. "What's going on?" he asked. "Where you been all night?"

"What?" Isabel called up, her arms crossed above her head, afraid I would strike her.

"Left umpteen messages on Homeboy's cell."

"Lucas has my cell phone," I said. It was true.

"Lucas is in Charlotte at a gig. What is wrong with you? It's time. Come on."

"Who?" She asked this.

"Both of you. Lord, what took you so long? He's been holding on."

"He wants me," in a tiny voice. "I want to say goodbye." She had never said that, in all this time.

Late-sixties beach architecture in the Carolinas leaves a lot to be desired. There's the instability, especially in houses built way up on pilings which often wobble even in normal winds, and inside there are cheap materials throughout: fake wood paneling, veneer floors, aluminum trim. There's the ubiquitous and usually dysfunctional sliding glass doors. Everything is plain, nothing fancy. But then again the whole rationale for a double A-frame like that—the name was Seasite, I read the plaque by the door, as I let Isabel go in first—was to give people as much window to look out of as possible. Places like that give you the chance to forget there has to be a structure at all, that a building has to have walls and adjust to its setting, its lot, the geography, the junk around it. Just shelter in principle, the whole point being the view. In this case, the sliding windows worked fine. Bit, whom we found on the couch in the living room, carefully dressed and cared for, but like a broken bird shuddering under blankets, the IVs attached, hardly able anymore to breathe, asked me to open them so he could hear the ocean. As I did this, his mother sat down at his feet, and caressed them. A while longer, I don't know how long, he struggled, gasped. The dawn was just coming on and so everything in the room, which when we first entered was like twilight, turned more golden, more serious. From such flimsy windows, when you look out you almost feel as if you are in the waves, for the frame is meant to disappear. When I looked back, it wasn't the sad and tragic scene I had thought I would see. Harriet and her sister and his mother and Terry were hoisting him up, so he could see the light, which came up over the ocean and went right through the house then, to the back windows, and out.

That day in Tucumcari, when I was eleven, I went running among those men in the garden at the rehab hospital looking for my cousin. When you are young you love everyone in your family, and you know they really really love you. You have no doubt. He knew me right off, called out, "Hey. Over here." Of fifteen men he was the only one to call out like that. And I knew him right off, too: a beautiful black-haired man in that southwestern sun with blue eyes same as the sky, exactly. He looked hard at me, right into me, and I felt immediately that a whole lot inside me—all the stuff, all the pride, all the plans for reconstructing the man in the mesa—would have to step aside for his gaze—or dissolve. Bit's was a pure gaze, and I knew it then. He said my real name, which is Homer, which isn't Homeboy.

The illusion in such glass houses, such transparent houses, is that the light passes through everything, even the people in them, or at least that was the effect that day. It was something to behold. None of us cried for half an hour after, for the feeling when he looked at us, so fiercely conscious, so clear, was joyous, weightless, there was a glory about it. We all saw it. Even Isabel saw it, amazing as that is. That is all I have to say about it. Words would just get in the way of it, cloud it up. You have to let them go, even, they are the last thing, but you have to. He let his head go back and arched a bit, so he could be taken, and he was gone.

It was as if that one in me could see through the whole world, for a moment, and past it.

It was as if that's what Bit wanted me to hold on to, to keep.

Paradise

Homer "Homeboy" Cobb II, November 5, 2000

Half the town is talking already. The rest will read about it in tomorrow's paper. But I am not interested in why Uncle Tulip wants me arrested. A civil suit is a civil thing, he says, and this thing wasn't civil. Breach of contract, actually, would be civil, he's saying, *what Homeboy did was malicious, criminal.* I am interested in an ideal life. I am interested in telling you what it would be like, if you are curious.

There will be people of all types in the town of Fayton, and they will speak to each other. No one will covet. This whole material thing will be worked out from the get-go. Everybody is going to understand that things are alive before you have them but dead once you do, as I have come to realize. In the end they make your life not your own but their own afterlife, like things' heaven. You lose what soul you had, the more you have, unless you work with them, turn them into something new. In fact I may have known this all along. It would explain why I got into recycling.

My uncle Tulip was very put out when I first took up what he called junk dealing as a trade. I could have gone to work for him pouring slabs or framing new houses, after all. But right away, other builders were using my salvage. Then, more and more, Uncle Tulip's clients would want something old mixed in with the new. Dull tract house? Bring in some old heart pine flooring pilfered from a dilapidated place in Clarksboro or Sand Points, via Homeboy's of Fayton, Carolina's Finest. I was doing okay; our needs were modest. My wife, Paula, is not a material girl.

Then came the deluge, the mighty hand. Hurricane Horace, and with it, the five-hundred-year flood in October 1999. A fourth of the county underwater. Not for a few days—for a few months. The hogs were drowning in their slop—so were turkeys, chickens, all the manifestly dumb animals we raise here in awful conditions. The town of Alba Springs, what was left of it, had to be evacuated.

In the life in the realm of the ideal, which I share with Paula, we have three children who are ours and they are all pleased to be alive. We may eat bacon, but the pigs were once happy. Our children don't smoke when they are nine the way I did nor do they nearly die from how badly they want to leave this town like the generation right ahead of us. My children have all kinds of friends. What they drive and who their daddies are and what color are not the reasons they picked them. My children are not obese. They are not addicted to TV or computer games. They run and they swim and they like the backyard, and they go into everybody's if they feel like it. They are occasionally barefoot. Their parents actually love them and want them, do right by them—this most of all, most of all. The firstborn of my children is a little boy named Archie. He is whole; he has every part.

This business—my conceivable arrest—started with something Paula said. During one of those slow, unelectrified Horace afternoons, the world on pause, she turned to me: "I'm ready, Home." (Sometimes she just calls me "Home.")

Let me explain. Up until the days of Horace, she had never been ready. She worries a lot. She has reason to. She teaches second grade in the city schools, which are no longer integrated because the white people have run. So once she said she was willing to bring one more Cobb into this morass, let me say, it was a new day around here.

It's a fundamental you want the best for your child, don't you know. That's not being sentimental, that's not special pleading. I decided to get serious, or what I thought was serious.

About seventy days later, when the Alba finally sank back into its rightful banks, I went down to see what had really happened at that end of the county. Emergent from the formless mud, the only true landmark left for a hundred miles around: the old Alba Springs Hotel, caked, coated, bloated and half-ruined by river sludge. Still grand, though: Eastlake bric-a-brac on the porch, late Victorian stained glass in excess. Alba Springs was called Fay-tonville in the 1820s, before everybody decided to get up and move to the railroad, and escape the malaria at the river and the more common every-year floods, and drop the "ville." This was where our first people settled—the English, the Scots, the Irish, the Huguenots, the African slaves, and the Quakers, who were always doing what they could to buy back the African slaves, and free them. Here, there had once been something to look out over, a prospect, and good water from wells, and a way to get to the Atlantic by raft or small craft. After people had moved to where Fayton is now, they remembered the old place. In the 1900s they came back, and sat on the veranda of the Alba Springs, when the fashion was to take the waters, to get a taste of the old life, take a cure, go to the origin, the genesis.

It was a sad day down at the Springs. Not only were all the beautiful old buildings rotting, and the people still gone; the wells themselves were bad. The hog slop flooding into the water table had ruined them for a generation, according to the state health department. The Hawkins family were going to have to close down their artesian bottling business, the only real concern left in the village.

The very same day I saw these ruins, I came home and Paula told me the news. A blue circle, a hit. This convergence was a sign, the first of several.

The DA in Fayton is Tamara Johnson Lemoine. She went to Duke and then Georgetown. She could have gone anywhere to practice—smart woman, near perfect score on the bar. She decided to come back here and see what she could do about keeping Fayton County lawful, or perhaps, I secretly hope, just. She is dark and short. She has small calves and healthy thighs. Her eyes are beautiful and wide apart and she has a good husband, Lucian, who works in computers up near Oleander in the Piedmont. She wears very bright blouses, gold or leaf green, which shine underneath her black suits. Lawyers who go up against her, white men of Uncle Tulip's generation, call her a spitfire. I don't think she wants to arrest me, for she has been dragging her feet until today. There is the issue of grand larceny, though—she mentioned it the first time she called this morning, around nine.

We don't live in the right world, we live in this one where certain people want to play a lot of golf and have other people carry their clubs. I knew that from the start, but I was intrigued just the same when Uncle Tulip called me, said he'd had a talk with old man Hawkins. I said I had a talk with him too. That beautiful hotel, I said, somebody should save it. "Just what I was thinking," Uncle Tulip said. He had heard our news, he said, congratulations, and by the way, given my new situation in life as a father-to-be, maybe I'd like to go in with him?

He had already bought the whole complex on the promontory:

hotel, springhouses, outlying buildings, summer cottages, even the chapel. He had a grand plan: "Alba Springs Landing" about five miles from the real one, in the middle of a cotton field. The first gated community in Fayton County: golf course and security cards and black women in little kiosks with guns in their holsters to keep away the riffraff. Fake lake. It wasn't really reconstruction. It was reconceiving, taking apart the old hotel and other structures, using the elements. A porch column here, a stained glass window there.

"But who is it for?" Paula asked me when I described it to her. I ignored her. Uncle Tulip had made a huge gesture, and he had in mind making me rich, rich along with him, of course.

"No, you have the wrong idea," I told Paula. "There's going to be condos for the middle income, patio lots."

"Well, could we live there?" she asked. "People like us?"

The answer was no, we both knew, but I thought she'd come around. I threw myself into that mud, and the wood underneath it. There was work to be done: dismantling, hauling, stripping, sanding. We took crews of grown-up disabled people that the Goodwill has waiting for a job, sat them down at long tables in an old tobacco warehouse up in Clarksboro, and gave them the tools and the putty, the strippers and the fine sandpaper. A "sheltered workshop."

As the first month, then the second, went by, I told Paula maybe we could move out there—Tulip would give me a good loan. We would have it all like it used to be, long time ago, before I was even born, I started to believe. Like they say the fifties were. I was not around for the fifties. Our child would ride his bike down to the new clubhouse, which would look something like the old hotel, except for a few strategic changes, like the black ladies in the kiosks, and the golf trails, and the festival marketplace, and so on.

"What festival?" Paula said. "What's got into you?"

The paper called it the "largest salvage operation in the history of the state." Said it was like those folk parks they do in Europe, take all the indigenous architecture and put it in one open-air museum. I showed her the article. But she was more cranky by the day, asked me what folk park requires a pat-down upon entry.

March, April, Paula didn't rest up like they say to do your first trimester. She took on afternoon tutoring—thirty children on free school lunches don't know their colors, can't write their names. She wanted to get them caught up before her maternity leave. When she came home I'd be het up about what Uncle Tulip's architects were planning, how cute the landing was going to be.

But one night in May, she listened for quite a long time, then said, "Why won't you just look at me?"

"I can't take my eyes off you," I said. I liked how big she was getting. I thought she was beautiful. I couldn't get her out of my mind. I still can't. Her lips were a little thicker, which was not bad. Actresses these days pay a lot of money for thick lips, I told her.

Then I went on about the plaster ceiling medallions. One original had fallen apart in my hands that very day, so we were making molds with polymer resin, very delicate work.

"I didn't mean how I look, Homeboy," she said. "I meant why are you so obsessed—?"

"I'm just trying to make us some money, get us a new life," I said.

"It isn't something you get. It is something you invite," she said.

"We can't raise the baby here," I said. I meant in our little house on our street which had started to look sad to me, not good enough. We live downtown and everybody around us is old, closed up inside, don't like to come out, as if they are ashamed. Old Mr. Stark, the druggist across the street, for one example, hadn't been outside in six months. I look in on his sad place every now and then.

"Why not?" she said. "You, and you don't get it." And I heard that faithless thing she has inside her. That why-do-anything thing. She went over the stories in my family, in hers. My uncle Archie who killed himself, my cousin Benedict who had a hard life, took heroin, etc. My grandfather was a famous drunk. "Look at all this too long nobody would ever be born," she said.

I said don't say that. I made my plea.

She took my cheeks in her hands and said, "And you. I never knew this about you. Now? I'm stuck with you." And she went outside to sit under the pecan tree and cried her eyes out. She wouldn't let me comfort her.

In my ideal life, people know what they are doing all the time. This knowledge flows into them, they grab onto it, because it is good, the reason. They never get obsessed with the wrong things for the right reason. I told Paula about this, this morning.

That was after Tamara, the DA, called the second time. About three hours ago. She wanted to know could I come in for a talk? She said, "Perhaps we could consider taking it down. What about that, for a compromise?"

I wanted something else from her.

"Oh, Homeboy, what a mess this is," Paula said. "Give it back to Tulip."

"You hate Tulip," I said.

"No," she said. "*Hate* isn't the word."

Let me explain. When school let out and Paula could slow down, I thought she'd come around. After all, women want stuff, I reasoned, deep down, no matter what they say they want. That's why men pile it up.

Every night, if I tried to go through the highlights of work, she always stopped me, and said something like, "What have we gotten ourselves into?" And then she'd waddle out to the pecan tree again. I finally had to tell somebody. I chose Uncle Tulip. Maybe I should have known better. He said it was hormones. He said women are horrible when they are pregnant, crazy and screechy like cats who have eaten lead chips. He asked if I'd ever found one under a porch the summers I used to sand and paint old houses. He was eager to go on with his comparisons. I begged him to stop.

When school kicked in around August 10, I told Paula it was too hot, she should take off. She wouldn't listen. August 15, I got a call from the hospital, said she'd been admitted with bleeding. She'd been in the cafeteria moving some tables so the children could finish their mural. It was week twenty-three—the baby was about the size of a Cornish hen.

She was in there three days. We were given several scenarios. Some good, some not so. RX: complete bed rest when she got home. I drove to Clarksboro and got her mother. The two of them fled to the upstairs bedroom with the strongest air conditioner. I had to stay downstairs on the couch, awaiting reports from above. When asked, I set off on my small missions to procure what was needed before our boy would set his tiny foot here. The prescriptions were strange to my ears, like the things voodoo gods require, they say: *rice and beans, raw mashed coconut, fresh blood of a sheep, shredded yarn, fingernail clippings.* In the Other Realms there is apparently no accounting for taste. Here was Paula's and Archie's list: *Tim Robbins movies, Shredded Wheat Unsalted (no icing), blackberry tea, frozen cranberries, Pet Milk, California King feather pillows, Kleenex, Cheerios, huge bras, tight socks, sheets, towels, crosswords in thick books, cold lemon ice.* There had to be more I could do. I prayed on it.

I told Uncle Tulip again how helpless I felt one morning, opened my heart to him. I was terrified this baby wasn't going to live, or would come to us partly broken.

I got a piece of his mind. He seemed delighted to give me his sage observations, what a long life of watching football and putting everybody else in construction for a radius of fifty miles out of business had revealed to him about Nature needing to take its course, about the wisdom of survival of the fittest.

My mind went clear and blank: cold gray. I felt blindsided, struck.

Later in the afternoon, when I was dismantling the last of the Springhouse Number Two, though, it came to me in a flash.

Almost September. Our twenty-fifth week. It shouldn't be an amazing thing, should it, for an unlatched door to swing out into the open air. My men, Gerry McCabe and Randy Beech, were hauling out the front one, frame and all, though, and the thing just opened. Through it I saw something new. The woods were that late summer color, that green that puts you in mind of black, or charcoal, even. But still everything seemed fresh: the river winding sultry in her banks, the cliff and trees draped in eager vines. The world lifted up her skirts, let down her hair, for just a moment.

I knew exactly what to do.

Her third call this morning, Tamara said I had missed my appointment. "I want you to know I can come pick you up, Homeboy," she said. "In a New York minute."

"Tulip can take it down," I said to her. "He owns the whole damn town. He bought the church right out from under the citizens."

"It is a ghost town, Homeboy," she said. "Everybody there took the insurance and left," which is not what she said a couple of days ago, when I confessed.

The afternoon I had my vision, I went by the sheltered workshop and picked up the door and two stained glass windows, put them in the back of my truck. They were clean down to the bare wood. Hundred years' worth of paint on them gone. You could see where the carpenters marked some of the two-by-fours with chalk to price them, or tell their helpers where to put them.

I drove out there and I put down two stained glass windows from the original hotel where they had been to start with, and framed them up. To this, to fill in, a few days later, I added some clapboard siding, and then two more windows, fresh from the workshop.

I propped it all up with simple braces in the back. A facade, is all it was. A facade without the complications of a whole building. An elaborate, beautiful gate, with sets of doors, and windows, and bric-a-brac, and a few gables, to be accurate. I kept adding to it at night, in the afternoons when I could get away. I put in some personal touches, maybe got carried away—I carved a few birds, I added an eagle I'd gotten from a bank up in Wilmington, some pews, some wooden ladies who'd once stood in a bar at North Salter at the Steel Pier, the old brackets that held up my grandma's porch before Tulip redesigned the place. There was some beauty to it, I thought, a private beauty. Nobody knew of it but me. At home, my mother-in-law's macaroni, Paula lying on her side, scared as all get out, saying she was crazy to attempt this at thirty-seven.

"Look at my hands," she said—they were swollen, so were her ankles, and her cheeks. But I could tell her it was going to be okay. I knew it. I was building our spell, our gate, our way through. His way in.

It didn't take Tulip long to notice. He went after the Goodwill, said those losers couldn't keep track of their own mess, much less

his windows and doors and pillars. Wanted to know why I was giving them a job. Gerry was his next target. My uncle searched all
over the county. He read the inventories from auctions in Oleander, Columbia. His architects were going crazy, ordering new
items to the old specifications. They said they wouldn't get the
same woods, the same workmanship. It never occurred to Tulip to
go back to the Springs. Or to ask me what I knew. He assumed I
knew nothing.

He has always assumed that.

Couple of days ago, Tamara called and said some people had
phoned her. They had been down to Alba Springs to be baptized
by the pastor of the Full Immersion Free Will Baptist Church her
mamma used to belong to. Somebody was building on that old
cliff, looked like the hotel, but crazy-like, windows and a patch-
work, all with brand-new wood, or what looked like brand-new
wood. It was just the front, no sides. What did I know about this?
Was it an outsider artist?

They were just here about ninety minutes ago: Constable Baldwin, and Tamara. I wouldn't come to them, so they came to me.
They had a proposition, gave me a "little while" to decide. If I will
go back, take it down and give it to its rightful owner, then she will
tell him he's been made whole and there will be no charges. If he
wants to go further, it will be a civil matter. Breach of contract, etc.
Failure to deliver, etc. Nothing criminal. "Why doesn't *he* go?" I
asked her. "Uncle Tulip can take it down, it's hardly tacked up,
would collapse in a strong wind."

"Homeboy? He's hurt," she said. "He brought you in as a part-
ner, his own nephew. You stole. He's trying to get his subdivision
built. Look at it from his perspective."

"It's more than a subdivision. It's a concept community," I said.
"He thinks he's building a town—he doesn't know the difference."

It was just day before yesterday, we drove out there, Tamara and I. She was the first to lay eyes on it, after me and the Full Immersion people. It's rather handsome now, if I do say so. I've been working about six weeks. She admired it, certainly. She also said it was a beautiful spot, that's why her mother's people always went there for homecoming, and baptisms, for their church used to be down at the end of town where the cliffs are lower, way long time ago. Her mother's family were slaves bought and freed by the Quakers at Quaker Bank. The first church was there, she said, washed away by the early high water, the one that sent people scurrying up to the railroad, but the elders still remembered.

I told her about my ideal life. She agreed with me. Alba Springs Landing wasn't any real improvement—in fact, it was more of the same, only worse. I said, imagine if we could go back, all the way back, and start over, and get it right. To here, to the original settlement. She told me the eighteenth century wasn't far enough back. I agreed, things couldn't be as they were then, not some below the cliff and some above, not some on one side, and some on the other. No masters, no slaves. In fact, she set me straight about just about any version of the past I could come up with, until we got back to Eden, then we had to deal with the snake. And she pointed out the whole thing would have to be flood-proofed, up on piers this time, set back. The cliff was washed out some from underneath. If we did that, I said, I'd clear the trees to keep the vista. She pointed out it would be a problem, that we'd have to wait fifty years before we could use the artesian springs again. I came up with ways to work around that, catch rainwater, collect dew. I thought we had a pretty good time, that we had reached an understanding.

Apparently not. But it doesn't matter, really.

Because, the next morning—this would be yesterday morning—the doctors told Paula she could get up. It was the end of her thirty-fifth week. Her swelling was down, and the baby was out of danger. They peeked in on him, gave us a full report. He is healthy, big, ready.

She knew Uncle Tulip had been snooping around, asking questions, trying to ferret out the thief. She had started to suspect, but she had no real idea. I waited until sunset. We carefully walked out to the car—her first ride in weeks and weeks—and drove up the mud road Uncle Tulip's men had bush-hogged, and turned in to the old wide place where the wagons used to pull in. I told her to cover her eyes. When I said she could uncover them there it was—my spell, my wall of Paradise. She saw the beauty, I know it. But then, she said, "Why did you do this? For me?" And I didn't answer her, I just got her to go through that beautiful old hotel door, which I placed in the exact middle.

In an ideal world, she would have been so happy she would have had the baby right there, that minute. No hard labor, just presto. In an ideal world, a man doesn't get arrested for trying to do right by his wife, make his new baby feel welcome. In an ideal world, people aren't still waiting, and waiting, and waiting around for the joy to arrive, the perfection to commence. It's already here, at the door, poised and banging to come through, instead of Tamara Johnson Lemoine and Constable Baldwin for the second time in one day. In an ideal world, Paula wouldn't have tried to stop me last evening on that rise, to say, "Home, take it down, this is not the ideal world."

But she was smiling when she said it, I saw her. So from that, I gauge the time must be approaching, we must be very close.

Should a man be put in jail for such results?

Where What Gets Into People Comes From

Lily Stark

As soon as they walked into the Cobbs' home that morning, Lily's mother said the facts of the man's murder were too horrible to repeat. But Lily's father insisted a story as awful as how Mr. Homer was slaughtered would teach Lily something about this world.

"I don't care about the world you even mean," Lily said.

For a long time Lily had been looking for a cause for her wildness. She'd just found it. So she felt like she could tell her father off. And they were in front of neighbors, so he wouldn't slap her. Old man Homer Cobb had been murdered in the most degrading way imaginable. There were thirty or forty people standing around, some in line with the Starks, waiting for the coconut cake, others over with Methodist ladies in navy blue crepe dresses pulling out their small handkerchiefs, giving condolences to the Cobbs' living children. There were men and boys in between, staring out, eating deviled eggs off glass plates. It was 1967, a small town on the Carolina border. Lily Stark was fifteen. She could hardly stand being alive. Earlier that day at the Cobbs' plot, Lily had noticed the headstone of Mr. Homer's first son, Archie, who had died the day she was born. June 12, 1952, when he was twenty-seven years old. Lily had lived across the street from the Cobbs her whole life, but she had never known there was an Archie.

As soon as they had come back to the home, Lily had gone to ask Sidney, who had been hired for the day to serve the food for the mourners and wash up. She worked for lots of families, but was between jobs at that time. She knew things that went on in all the white people's houses. She said that when Archie Cobb got home from the war back in 1948, he took a job at a state hospital outside of town "to be near the dope." By and by Archie fell for a nurse who saw his withered thigh where he'd found the veins. She wouldn't have him. And he could not be consoled by the Lord or any person, so Archie took his mother's Nash to the cliffs over the Alba at the Springs, drove off the edge, and crashed it to tiny pieces. Died like that. It was hot for June, too hot.

"I was born then," Lily said.

"I know," Sidney said.

Archie must have had a second thought as his mamma's car was tumbling down to the river and he came flying out, spirit only, flesh doomed, and there was my mother, pregnant in that heat, sitting outside in a hammock right across the street from the Cobbs'. Archie dove right into my girl baby body. I have his soul, so Lily thought.

If somebody had offered her morphine that spring, she would not have thought twice about trying it. Archie had been a reckless man. She herself was a reckless girl. He just wanted to get out. He hadn't made it. So it was Lily's destiny to leave: she'd known this since she was little. This even explained why her mother couldn't stand her—her mother always said the Cobbs were low. And Lily had no respect for the solid things in life, to hear her father tell it. That was what he wanted to teach her, as it was what life had shown him. But Lily saw the beauty instead in the flight of Archie's soul over town because of the terribleness of lost love, hoping to leave and looking to land at the same time. She adored the image of poor Archie overhead, she could even feel how the sky felt, the soft heat of the heavens. Then she told her father what she thought of the world he meant.

He said: "Listen to me. You mind what can be seen, touched, counted, otherwise—"

"What?" she asked, not really caring to know, not anymore. "Why didn't anybody ever tell me about Archie Cobb, how he died? The day I was born? Nobody ever tells me what I need to know." She knew she'd infuriated him now.

"You want to end up like Homer Cobb? Or his son?"

Lily refused to see the parallel. She stood there, in line for the coconut cake. She knew what she knew. What mattered.

• • •

In eastern Carolina the land appears at first too low and dull for any feature as remarkable as a deep river and a steep drop, so the cliffs over the Alba are a shock. But when you follow the folds of the plain from where the Alba starts to its destination—past the promontory at the Springs, down towards the deeper rivers, into the Atlantic, it's clear that what at first seems overly dramatic for that landscape in truth cannot be helped.

Fayton was a town like other towns on that plain, so small all kinds of people were close at hand. There were twelve houses total on the block of Winter between Park and Locust, one mansion, several proud Queen Annes with towers, and the rest little houses, like the Starks' place and the Cobbs'. People lived in each other's porches and backyards and parlors then. There was some vigilance, but sooner or later every secret saw the light.

Lily's father's house and the Cobbs' right across from it started out in the twenties as plain bungalows, white frame and mute, raised on piers with seven stairs up the front and thick half-brick pillars which supported the roof of the porch. They each had two gum ball trees in their yards, and across the street and on the corner where the McKenzies lived there were brick walls. These were finer houses with generous gardens which were opened each spring so everyone else could peep into them, and wish.

When he was young Homer Cobb was slender but muscled, dark, considered handsome. In high school in the early twenties, he liked to act in plays. Eventually he became a salesman. He bought the house on Winter after he married in 1921. This was during the days when people thought the town of Fayton would amount to something: a ten-story building was put up, two five-and-dimes were built, then a hotel with an imposing lobby. There was a bus station, a train station with a train that came into it and left for Danville, Virginia, and three cab companies. Mr. Homer was excitable, but he was a working man. Up to a certain point in his life, he was an Elk, a Methodist, a fair earner, a charmer, a good father.

Mrs. Geneva, his wife, was once a nurse but she had given it up to raise her boys. She was a kind woman with a sweet tooth, stout, and a great baker. Her specialty was big white cakes. She used boiled icing, the kind that hardens and makes of a cake a monument. The hair about her head was cotton candy. There were burst veins in her cheeks. Archie was Mrs. Geneva's first son, born 1925, and the best-looking. His hair was dark and slightly curly. His chin had a dimple. Tobias, who came much later, in 1933, was stout, after his mother's side. He had a winestain between his nose and his mouth, so people called him Two-lip, then Tulip. His whole life he would never get rid of the name. The third boy, Honey, was a change-of-life baby, born during the Second War, 1944. He had wild red hair. Soon as he was walking all of Winter Street said there was something wrong with him.

In 1952, when he was nineteen, after his brother died, after his daddy set out upon his second life, Tulip Cobb eloped with Isabel Odom, runner-up to homecoming queen, who was pregnant. Her people were mill workers—a generation back, they'd owned land, but they lost everything in the thirties. She still believed she had married down. So she got Tulip to make her promises.

Tulip's worst flaws were his weakness for his mother's cakes and the fact that he went after his living brother with whatever was near at hand—a belt, a big shoe, a plank of wood. He believed in the beating. Honey had to be tamed, it was true—anything in the world might get into him. The boy shot at birds with BBs from his own little blind in the backyard, and he missed, killing squirrels, terrorizing the neighborhood dogs and cats. He came sneaking around after Lily Stark and her friends in the yard, with a garter snake dangling from the handle of a hoe. Mrs. Geneva never intervened, on either side, Tulip or Honey. That was what living with men was like, she said. Stop them from one thing they will do something else, pretend it is the opposite, but it will be just as bad.

Through the early years, the fifties, due to her father's efforts and her mother's demands, Lily Stark's family's bungalow took on dormers, and wrought iron like people had in New Orleans so it didn't match Mrs. Geneva's exactly anymore. Her mother got creeper with little leaves to cover the grassless yard because she said she couldn't stand the sad sight of that white Carolina soil. It wasn't even soil. It was sand.

All this time the Cobbs' got shabbier. It sorely needed paint, repairs to the porch. But it turned out that the fact the two houses looked less and less alike had no effect whatsoever upon Homer Cobb and his ways.

Long after midnight one night when she was four years old Lily came downstairs for water and saw the front door was open. Tulip Cobb was standing just beyond the screen under the yellow bug light. It was a summer without air-conditioning, only fans. The Starks didn't keep their windows closed or their doors locked. Nobody did. Lily's father finally let Tulip in, but still for a while they stood there looking at something, not doing anything. Tulip's striped pajamas were turned over at the waist. Lily could see the exhausted elastic. He had stubble on his round face, and ashy hair that fell into his wide blue eyes. Tulip had moles. All the Cobbs had moles.

Eventually Lily put her head around to see what the two men saw: on her mother's slip-covered couch against the wall lay Homer Cobb half-curled up in a ball, his head thrown back at an angle, his mouth open, snot puddled on his upper lip. Her mother was going to be furious, furious. Her housekeeper, Pauline, would be upset too. Tulip, who was large so people assumed he was strong, assumed he could play football well, for example, when the fact was he couldn't, made the first move. He lifted his daddy's head, then reached under the arms, and dragged him down, causing the body to unfurl on her mother's wall-to-wall carpet. Mr. Homer would wake up, Lily hoped. She came out from hiding, and her daddy didn't see her, but Tulip looked right at her. He was in awful pain, she could see that. Tulip was married, but he was not a real daddy like Lily's, he was not one who had been through the war, seen action in the Pacific, suffered, bled, saved people's lives and had his life saved. Tulip didn't have a store like Lily's daddy did. Tulip was a teenage father with barely a job at a gas station and a father in the wrong living room and he lived in a tired house the shame of the neighborhood and in his face even Lily could see how terrible he felt even to exist.

Finally Lily's father stepped forward, and took Mr. Homer's limp ankles. With Lily's father moving forwards, Tulip going backwards, they carried Mr. Homer, whose arms hung down on his sides, across the porch, down the stairs, over her mother's creeper, across the Cobbs' dirt yard. At the other end Mrs. Geneva was holding the door open. For all the disturbance nobody said very much. The next morning Lily's father said Mr. Homer didn't care anymore about who he was or what he was, didn't give a damn, always had been a dreamer. Now he was worse.

Isabel's first child was Benedict, whom everybody called Little Bit, then just Bit. Four years later she had a daughter, Dora. Even with two children, they still all lived in that house, but they needed more money, so Tulip went to work selling cars for the Ford dealer.

In 1958 Lily's mother hired one of the brilliant gardeners who worked across the street to set in rows of bulbs in her backyard that took turns blooming, and azaleas and behind them flowering plum trees. They built an arbor for grapes. In March Isabel invited herself over with Dora and Bit to sit on a blanket, and Lily joined them. Claire McKenzie, the little girl who lived in the big house on the corner, came over too, with cookies. Pauline came out of the kitchen with iced tea. It felt like everybody's garden. Lily was conscious of spring, of the beauty. She said to herself, I am alive. I am six years old.

Isabel seemed proud when Tulip started moonlighting doing home additions, small jobs. He paid a crew to paint his parents' house. Crisp, sharp white. Green shutters. Wood houses were white then; it was like a law. You didn't have anything too grand, too gaudy; it might make people covet. Tulip was finally making some money.

When she was only seven Lily started wondering about God, what he could possibly have been thinking. Her father's father had been a preacher, a poor man, some people said crazy. Her mother said crazy. Her father always took her to church. Her mother wouldn't go. Lily was bored by most of the ceremonies and the sermon but there was something about praying.

Every so often Mr. Homer would still stumble into the Starks' in the middle of the night, and Lily's daddy would call next door. When Tulip came over, that was all Lily saw of Tulip. He was selling cars or he was doing renovations those days, working day and night. Eventually Tulip put in a walkway of slate around the side of the Cobbs' house leading to the rear, and installed a light. After that, Mr. Homer slept it off on the back porch, not in the Cobbs' house proper. He mostly stopped showing up at the Starks'.

That same year Tulip took a few lots at the edge of Fayton, next to nothing, cheap land, other side of the train tracks, and built three little houses on speculation. They were all alike, with choppy yards and few trees. People bought them right up.

Mr. Homer took up drinking with white cab drivers whose records were so bad they could only work for the colored cab company. He went with the men who ran numbers and moonshine and made deliveries for the homegrown gangsters, men left over from Prohibition, white men and Indian men and light-colored colored men who wore boots and hats even inside a store. Sometimes they wore their old striped suits from the thirties, so they looked like people in the TV show *The Untouchables*. Everybody had a TV by that time, although some had been quite reluctant. Many said it was a fad and would pass, not to take it to heart.

Lily started walking to the library by herself when she was eight. It was in an old house way downtown. She read about religions there. She liked the Christian heresies. She read that she lived in a fallen world. The ones who made it hadn't got it right, and they were falling or fallen too, and terribly sorry about it. She could see that, it seemed the only explanation. She read how everything has its cause in the soul's life. She practically memorized the *Encyclopedia of Superstition*: in Bohemia when a person is dying they open a window. Let the ghost get where it's going. In the Baltic countries it is widely believed that animals always see the spirits of the dead.

That spring Lily could hear the Cobbs arguing if she lay awake at night. Isabel wanted to find a bigger house. Everybody could move, Mrs. Geneva, and Honey, the whole crowd. Mrs. Geneva said absolutely no. In the end they didn't do it. Isabel was furious. Tulip had to make it up to everybody. He bought his mother a dog, Cookie, whom Lily soon fell in love with. He promised Isabel a new, brick house, just for her, himself, and the kids, in a subdivision he was going to start, out across the highway. Everything spanking. He said he would borrow the money. Become a real developer. Then they would move. Isabel said if he didn't keep his word she would leave him for another man. She said she had plenty of offers.

. . .

Christmas 1962 Mrs. Cobb sent over three pounds of pecan divinity in a tin, so Lily's father said they were calling on them. Her mother wouldn't go. Nothing was good enough that year for her mother. She'd gotten a Cadillac and didn't like driving it.

For a long time at the Cobbs' it was just Tulip and Lily's daddy, and Mrs. Geneva and Isabel and the children, and of course, Honey there impersonating a human being, Lily thought, a short clip tie on, a jacket with the sleeves too short. Honey was a topic all over Fayton by that time. He kept failing tenth grade, held the record, for one thing. He showed up in the middle of the night in people's yards, howling, sticking his face in their windows.

It was as if nobody thought of Mr. Homer as missing until he appeared in the archway by the dining room. He made a slow, tentative entrance. He had on a shirt and a coat as if he'd been to church—Lily knew he hadn't. He began looking around and saying sweet things to his grandchildren whom he reached for, but didn't truly touch. In the center was the tree with so many gifts Tulip had bought underneath. Mr. Homer said nothing, but there was a place for him on the couch, as far away from the tree as possible, and he seemed grateful for it. Mr. Homer took a chocolate Millionaire Lily's father had brought and chewed it with his mouth open, the way even older people did tobacco. Seeing Mr. Homer and how his clothes hung off of him made Lily notice Tulip had become a real fat man. Lily had heard at Sunday school that Mr. Homer was drinking with the hands from the bright-leaf tobacco warehouses who came through in August. He drank with oyster shuckers and flounder cleaners from the fish market, with men who worked around the bus station, which still did a fair business.

That spring Lily went through the Mr. Sender horror. She didn't even understand it. Then Pauline quit. Lily figured this out in the summer: you could get on a bus in Fayton and get off the very same one in New York City. It started in Savannah as a local—it went through Charleston, then all the way. After it reached the Virginia line, it was even an express. But whenever Lily charted it out, made plans to run away, something told her it couldn't be. Fayton was the sort of town, when you were in it, there was no way out. People you met believed this even though they would agree a person might leave if you asked them twice. The truth made no difference in the long run, though, to what people believed.

In seventh grade, she made a new plan. Boarding school. She was rough—she needed finishing. They weren't going to send her, so she could shut up, her mother said. The girl on the corner, Claire McKenzie, was going. "But she has no mother," Lily's mother said. "Neither do I," Lily said. "I'll finish you," her mother said.

Tulip and Isabel were building their dream home by then, something other people thought was a marvel. Lily's mother was thinking about one too, and on Sundays they'd drive out into the county, and look at land to buy. He bought maps of every inch of Fayton County.

The year Lily became a teenager, something went right. The army took Honey. After that Tulip and Isabel and Bit and Dora moved across the highway, into their mansion which was up on a clay rise in Tulip's new subdivision. People were amazed by it: a huge brick negotiation between a ranch and a Georgian with a wide yard and large rooms all on one floor. Lily went to see it. The kitchen had thick-doored cabinets, all milled and built up and stained, not painted. There were exposed brick walls in the den, and a new sort of wood floor, plastic-shiny, and central air conditioners, not in the windows, outside the house. The inside Formica was inspiring in its way, as was the sunken pit for watching the TV. Dora told Lily her grandmother couldn't ever leave that house in town because she was worried her grandpa wouldn't find his way home if she moved. Dora thought this was a secret.

• • •

After six months, the army sent Honey back. Mrs. Geneva took him in. She had Cookie, she said. He'd never do anything to his mother. He was worse than ever, wrecking cars, spending time with dangerous people. When he was bored he ran outside naked in the daytime holding his BB gun, doing a rebel yell: it took a lot to get Lily's attention by the time she was in eighth grade. She went over and told Mrs. Geneva to get him to stop. Mrs. Geneva's lips trembled a little—she was trying to keep from smiling. Lily attempted to imagine what was in Mrs. Geneva's mind, behind her little teeth. Tulip tried putting Honey in an apartment, but Honey came home to his mother after a few weeks. What was he going to eat?

Lily heard tales from the wild boys she french-kissed and went half the way with. Mr. Homer was riding the rails, camping out with the hobos, carrying on. As far as Lily knew Mrs. Geneva never filed a report on her husband. She never kicked him out formally. She never refused to let him come home to his hammock.

Once Mr. Homer stayed gone for two months straight. Then, it was a morning in January, when Lily went to get Cookie to take a walk, that the old man shocked her, more a ghost by then than a person, nearly bald and long-jawed, sleeping on the floor of the back porch. She sat there, listening to his thready breathing, watching him so long he started to look innocent. She was fourteen then, nearly grown. She remembered him that way, after.

When Mr. Homer woke he saw Tulip's workmen fixing the door screen. He told them to go to hell. What was the use, he said. He always cursed his son's crews. Nevertheless, piece by piece, Tulip had completely renovated the exterior of the house. He had destroyed the original front porch on piers and lowered it to the ground. Instead of the half-brick California bungalow pillars he put up plain, stained wood columns. He had painted the house Williamsburg green, which was daring. He rebuilt the porch from concrete, and sealed it. The whole front looked rather stately. Even Lily's mother admitted it: Tulip had managed to make Mrs. Geneva's house seem older, and also newer, and larger, and more imposing, than Lily's house. But when you were inside, nothing had changed: Mrs. Geneva's afghans, her rocker, and her old kitchen stove.

That next summer Lily's mother announced they were really going to get away from that place. She had two decorators, an architect. Start over from scratch. A new life. Where? Lily asked, full of hope. They'd go out in the country, away from it all. Moving, which everybody was doing, was a piss-poor excuse for getting out, she said to her mother. Her mother told her to leave her sight. Let me go, Lily said. Let me go, really go.

• • •

By the next April, Honey had got a girl pregnant. She was gritting her teeth and marrying him, so Honey took a job banging nails into two-by-fours for his rich brother. Mrs. Geneva had found out she had diabetes—she had to stop baking. Cookie barked at things that weren't there, because he was blind, people thought.

Mr. Homer had been away for one of his extra-long stretches. It was a day right after Easter, around noon, that Cookie, who was sleeping on the new brick front porch where it was cool, suddenly woke up and went around the back of the house in the waddling way he had been walking lately. He started barking at Mr. Homer's empty hammock. Mrs. Geneva opened the door for him. But Cookie didn't come into the kitchen to eat, his custom. Neither Mrs. Geneva nor Lily could get him off the subject of the hammock for the longest time.

Two days later the police found Homer Cobb's body in a warehouse in the oldest part of downtown, near the abandoned train station. His companion had risen up and beat Homer Cobb about the head until he died.

This took many blows, with a heavy weapon. When people heard the story, what was peculiar to them was that Mr. Homer hadn't run home, when he was only twelve blocks from his own house. The coroner said he'd been awake for the first five or ten hits. And he was dehydrated, but not drunk.

Homer Cobb's companion left him there to die, in that makeshift encampment where they were living to drink. He took to the rails. They found him in Saltfort by the docks. Every name he gave was an alias.

• • •

The weapon was one detail Lily's father held onto. He came back to the murder, that night, after the funeral, after Lily had already told him off once, demanding to hear about Archie the suicide. Her father said the murder was evidence of how far a man could fall, and evidence of this sort, which was ubiquitous when he was a boy, had become rarer and rarer in those days. This was the sixties, and everybody was losing his way. Mr. Homer's murder illustrated that ruin could be just blocks away from you—her father wanted Lily to see this point. Something had gone so terribly wrong with her. He'd worked hard to keep misery from her but that had drawn her to it: she was talking to crazy people, seeing the wrong boys, smoking cigarettes, being moody and lazy, planning to run off soon as she could.

She didn't need her father to serve her some misery, she said. Everything she saw in Fayton by then broke her heart. Like that girl going ahead and marrying Honey. Everybody, everybody, desperate to get out, incapable of leaving, of even seeing over the lip of this tiny, binding world.

Look at it, how bad it can get: a once handsome and lively man with a wife and three sons ends up killed the way someone might kill a cockroach, with the same sort of everyday and kitchen sort of instrument, a rather female instrument. The humiliation. It was a touchstone, a cautionary tale. Lily needed a dose of reality. Here it was. The man gave up, he gave in, he was swallowed. It can happen.

Lily said to her father, "Do you know what was in his mind?"

"His mind was gone," her father said. "What difference does his mind make?"

"He sat there for it. The coroner said so," she said.

"Look at it. In the face. The man failed at life," he said.

"How do you know?" she said.

"You have to have something to live for," he said.

"But all of this you put store by is going asunder some time. The vain things, things of this world. Mr. Homer knew that. You made me read that."

"You going to make that drunk a hero? Wise?"

"There must be something else," Lily said.

"Well, what is it? What is it?" her father said.

"Was everybody wrong before, to say there was something more?" she said. "What about your daddy?"

Her father looked at her as if she'd shot him. It was so rare that he looked at her at all, and here, when he did, she felt every side of his wound—it was unbearable.

The day Homer Cobb was going to die, the man who was with him asked for three dollars and twenty-eight cents for liquor. Homer had two dollars and a nickel. The man decided to take it out on him, the one dollar and twenty-three cents, so he picked up a cast-iron coffee pot lying there, and he hit him, again and again.

Early on, the pain got to be too much, so Homer let himself fly right out of his body, out a window, it felt like. He sort of watched the pain as it continued to come to him as a neutral phenomenon, a feeling of a certain heft and shape and breadth, but the fact that he was being hurt was something he couldn't identify with anymore. Instead he saw his second son, Tulip, his house up on that red knoll above the highway, attracting other big houses, and money like a magnet. And he saw Honey, a baby coming now, would he finally get himself attached to this earth, to practical life. He took a good long stare into that baby's face, the one who hadn't been born yet, Honey's child inside that poor girl. He tried to bless him. It occurred to Homer Cobb he was dying then, because he could see many things quite well, past and future. He knew that in ways his family would be relieved to see him go, and he didn't fault them for that, since he had failed so utterly, for so very long, to show his love for them by any other means.

With every one of the later blows, he saw a wider pattern, the Starks across the street, the fussy creeper in their yard, that house away-from-it-all they had decided to build, the Starks, the McKenzies, the Senders, all his neighbors. He saw all the people in Fayton—how the ones who were different were so close to the ones who weren't. He could hear Cookie barking then, loudly, full of mourning. The second-to-last one he saw was his wife, an inexplicable light behind her, standing in the kitchen door, which opened into that house Tulip had so cruelly disguised. So Homer let it be back the way it had started in the twenties, just a bungalow, modest and white, Geneva in the middle of everything, the source of everything, there holding one of her high white stiff cakes.

And then he turned around and saw something more, and beautiful, a place almost completely hidden from the ordinary world. He hadn't expected this, but soon as he saw it, he was sure it was where his first and dearest son had tried to coax the morphine to take him. Archie had made an error—it had never been a judgment.

A glimpse of this, and Homer let that go, finally, finally, finally, that burden he'd borne so long, his belief that his son had thrown away the life Homer had given him, because he found it worth so little. And then Homer paused, he had to pause, because of the sweetness, the sorrow, the relief—

These days, Lily saw when she returned, Tulip's project is almost complete. To find the residents of Fayton you have to circle around the edges, and seek out cul-de-sacs, and hidden grounds of his subdivisions, which form a defense against the old town, the abandoned, rotten parts. Besides a few old people, hardly anyone, of any class or race, lives downtown anymore.

Lily Stark turned out to be exactly what her father didn't want her to be. Except she was not a suicide but she thought of it in her twenties. She tried something else, and then something else— now she was a journalist, she wrote for magazines. She lived in Brooklyn with her second husband, her son. She turned her back, she invented herself new more than once. She never could take the tangible life very seriously, even while she longed for comfort.

When she got the call and had to go home, she knew she would grieve, but she didn't know it would feel like drowning. She kept remembering the way her father's face fell that day they buried Mr. Homer, the day she heard about Archie.

"You just want an escape," her father said to her finally after he recovered from looking like he'd been shot.

That was true. He had that right. "And what do you really want? Why do you always turn it into things?"

"Your mother wants them," he said.

"You have spent your whole life on them," she said. "Every hour."

"Why are you so cruel?" he said. "What made you like this?"

"You," she said.

Her father said nothing.

"Talk to me."

He wouldn't.

She slammed the door to her room, to contemplate the soul of Archie Cobb, the suicide.

. . .

After the ceremony, she went back to the old bungalow on Winter Street. The place was faded, with peeling paint, windows broken, no creeper in the yards. It was filled with junk—her father had lived there until the end, and he never threw anything away after his wife died. It was so bad she couldn't have the funeral reception there, as the custom was, years ago, at the Cobbs' house across the street. As soon as she walked inside the house, she remembered how she felt like dying for winning that day with her father, but it had been her father who died first.

. . .

Someone who came to her father's funeral told her that lately a few of the people who live in the developments have been saying something must be missing, maybe they should go back and live downtown. Maybe they could be inside each other's lives, and dwell in each other's secrets, share each other's living rooms and gardens, the way people say they used to do. As if they were kin. She recognized him. He was Honey's boy, a sane and decent man, impossibly. His name was Homeboy Cobb. He was really Homer the Second, the grandson. He had helped to take her father to the hospital when he had his last stroke, she'd heard. She thanked him. He mentioned he'd stay longer, but at the moment, he had a new baby, he'd have to get home. Then he returned to his subject—"Maybe we should all leave, start over instead, at the very beginning, I mean—" he said.

"There never was any leaving, never is," she said, but probably he didn't understand her, because she was speaking of her dreams: when they were serious she was always in Fayton, even though she was forty-eight years old, with her own history. She was still in that garden, where whatever she was before she was born came into her girl baby body. She was with her family or with Mrs. Geneva or Cookie or Bit or Dora or Mr. Homer or Tulip or Sidney or Pauline who raised her or Claire or with the wild boys she used to try to get to love her.

Just the night before Archie had appeared to her. He was hovering above, invisibly tethered to the garden, to the whole town, to the place at Alba Springs where he'd driven off, and he gazed upon it all with a longing which was the last thing he'd ever thought he'd feel, so it held him. He gestured toward the lands beyond the town's limits, the cliffs, the artesian springs, the rushing Alba, the ocean. Then he came so close he touched her shoulder, turned her around. What he showed her then startled her, woke her up: both their fathers staring back at them, inconsolable and amazed.